A Gangsta's Code 3

Lock Down Publications and
Ca$h Presents
A Gangster's Code 3
A Novel by **J-Blunt**

A Gangster's Code 3

Lock Down Publications
P.O. Box 870494
Mesquite, Tx 75187

Visit our website
www.lockdownpublications.com

Copyright 2019 by A Gangster's Code 3

First Edition April 2019
Printed in the United States of America

Lock Down Publications
Like our page on Facebook: Lock Down Publications @
www.facebook.com/lockdownpublications.ldp
Cover design and layout by: **Dynasty Cover Me**
Book interior design by: **Shawn Walker**
Edited by: **Lauren Burton**

Stay Connected with Us!

Text **LOCKDOWN** to 22828 to stay up-to-date with new releases, sneak peeks, contests and more…

Submission Guideline.

Submit the first three chapters of your completed manuscript to ldpsubmissions@gmail.com, subject line: Your book's title. The manuscript must be in a .doc file and sent as an attachment. The document should be in Times New Roman, double-spaced and in size 12 font. Also, provide your synopsis and full contact information. If sending multiple submissions, they must each be in a separate email.

Have a story but no way to send it electronically? You can still submit to LDP/Ca$h Presents. Send in the first three chapters, written or typed, of your completed manuscript to:

LDP: Submissions Dept
Po Box 870494
Mesquite, Tx 75187

DO NOT send original manuscript. Must be a duplicate.

Provide your synopsis and a cover letter containing your full contact information.

Thanks for considering LDP and Ca$h Presents.

J-Blunt

Prologue

In Starlight there was no such thing as turning down. Only up. And when it came to turning up, nobody did it like Super Trap. His cornrows hung just past his undefined shoulders; a diamond-studded money sign draped down to his stomach. His face was clean-shaven of any hair except a prepubescent mustache, and his eyes always shined bright. The hero's moniker always made people who had never met Trap do a double take. A shade under five-eight and lightly built, the caramel-skinned twenty-five-year-old looked harmless. His lifestyle was flashy. Jewelry. Expensive clothes. Exotic cars. Fast women. People flocked to Trap because he was young, black, and successful. And they knew any time Super Trap stepped onto a scene, there was no turning down. Only up.

"You think Dream goin'?"

D-Star looked at Super Trap, the scowl on his pockmarked face saying more than words. "Stop playin'. You know Semi baby momma off limits. That nigga crazy, and that bitch ain't stupid enough to fuck you and risk Semi findin' out."

Trap took a slow drink from the bottle of Aces, his eyes resting on the woman across the VIP section. Skin red as the setting sun and eyes that gleamed like stars in the night, Dream was every man's fantasy. She had long, curly black hair that had never been touched by a weave or extensions, seductive almond-shaped brown eyes, high cheekbones with a dimple on the right side, and lips that promised pleasure if a nigga ever got the chance. From the neck down she was an artist's perfect drawing. The way her G-cups spilled from the top of her dress made all her dresses look low-cut. Waist slim, hips wide, and an ass that would make a preacher sin, Dream was the embodiment of the word lust.

"You ever wonder what she was doin' to that nigga wit' her tongue?" Super Trap asked. "Semi do the most out here, but kept this nigga in line like he was her pit bull."

"Yeah, nigga. Key word is pit bull. Why you wanna know how she tamed a nigga who certified? If a bitch can do that to him, imagine what she'da do to you."

"You think he gon' beat that case?"

"It don't matter, nigga. What matter is Semi crazier than Beanie Segal in that movie *Paper Soldiers*. And his niggas ain't got no problems turnin' hoods into ghost towns."

"You act like I don't got shooters," Trap smirked, looking toward Opt, his day-one nigga and number one shooter.

"You would turn the city out over some pussy?" D-Star asked.

Super Trap laughed. "All I wanna know is how long her tongue is. Bitch look like a snake when she lick her lips. But I wouldn't cross that bridge in real life. Too much drama on the other side. But it ain't nothin' wrong wit' lookin'. That bitch bad!"

"Now you thinkin' like the nigga that turned a four and a split into a mansion," D-Star grinned. "And while you was wastin' yo' time starin' at M'dusa, I seen a flock of birds over there that ain't neva been in a Phantom or felt ostrich seats."

Super Trap and his squad partied and popped bottles into the wee hours of the morning. During the bash, Trap gave into his lower self and crossed Dream's bridge. A few smiles and bottles later, they exchanged numbers.

When the club closed, secret text messages brought their cars to the parking lot of a soul food restaurant. Dream leaned against her pink Challenger, the curves inside her Louis Vuitton dress giving the sports car a run for its money.

Trap swagged close, a smile on his lips and lust in his eyes. "They say lightnin' don't strike the same place twice."

She gave his words some thought. "I don't get it."

"A boss nigga and a boss bitch meeting is rare like lightning striking the same place twice."

Dream smiled at the clever remark. "That was good. Now I see what they be talkin' 'bout."

"Who is 'they', and what they say?"

"You know. People talk."

"Don't believe everything you hear. Most that shit be lies. Matter fact, don't believe er'thang you see, 'cause yo' eyes can lie to you, too."

She laughed. "You just full of line, huh?"

"Them ain't lines, sweetheart. Them mottos. I live by this shit. This how I stay up top. But enough 'bout me. Tell me 'bout you. Tell me what you like so I can make it happen for you."

"You movin' kinda fast, ain't you? You know who my nigga is. You bold."

"See it, want it, buy it, own it. Semi can't do nothin' for you. I heard he ain't got no bail. That nigga got his own issues. And since you met up wit' me, you realize you got needs. Let me take care of those."

Dream closed the distance between them, pressing her voluptuous body against his. Her tongue slipped between her lips, defying biology as it touched the tip of her nose and then down to her chin. "You know I'm a fire, nigga. Ain't you scared to get burned?"

Trap's hands found the soft flesh of her ass and squeezed. "I'm fireproof, shawty. Burn me up!"

The Hilton Hotel was ten minutes from the restaurant. During the drive, Trap's mind was so wrapped up in thoughts of Dream's tongue, titties, and ass that he didn't notice the black van following his Benz. When he got out of the car, tires screeched as the Dodge Caravan pulled to a stop in front of him. When the sliding door opened, an AR-15 stopped Trap from reaching for the pistol on his waist.

"Getcho bitch-ass in, fuck-nigga!" the man with the rifle growled.

Trap didn't move' fast enough, so the rough hands of another man snatched him into the van and took his pistol. When the passenger door opened, Dream climbed into the passenger seat.

"What this shit about?" Trap panicked.

"It's about you, Super Trap. It's always been about you. Semi bail is $200,000. We need that. We already got niggas at yo' house. They got yo' girl and yo' son."

Trap closed his eyes as the enormity of the situation dawned on him. He fell for the pussy trap and had no choice but to give up the money. "Okay. I'ma give y'all that shit. Just let my family go. I'ma make sure they don't call the police."

Dream smiled, happy with his cooperation. "Just give us what we came for and we gone."

***

Super Trap walked into his house and seen his girl sitting on the couch, their son wrapped in her arms. Across from them sat three goons holding automatic weapons. The sight pissed Trap off, and he spun to face Dream. Before he could get the words out, his eyes landed on a body on the floor near the hallway. It was Opt, his number-one shooter. Sadness swept through Trap at the death of his day-one.

"I told y'all I was gon' give up the money. Y'all didn't have to kill my nigga."

"You should be thankin' my niggas for that," Dream smirked. "They followed him here. Ask wifey 'bout that."

Even though the threat of death was all around, Trap felt the sting of jealously and betrayal as he looked toward his girl. "You was fuckin' my nigga?"

She looked away, unable to meet his eyes.

"Y'all can talk about that later," Dream interrupted. "Where that money?"

After giving his girl one more angry stare, Trap led Dream and two jack boys to the game room. Behind the wet bar was a secret compartment that hid a safe. Inside was more than enough to get Semi out of jail.

Dream spun to Trap. "This ain't personal, baby. But I gotta bring my nigga home."

Pow. Pow. Trap flinched as two gunshots echoed through the house. When he realized they came from the living room, his heart sank. Before he could fully wrap his mind around the loss of his family, Dream lifted a 9mm to his face and squeezed the trigger.

Chapter 1

The revving engine echoed through the night as Queenie kept most of her focus on the road while glancing at Born Ready out of the corner of her eye. Ha held the pistol loose in his grip, the bag of money at his feet.

"You know Pop not finna stop chasin' us. Y'all gon' have to settle this."

"What you think we finna do? Keep goin' where I tell you. Speed up and shut up."

Queenie followed his directions, checking the rear-view mirror to make sure Pop was still following in the Maserati. Instead of heading away from high traffic areas, Born Ready directed her to the more populated areas. Queenie decided to use it to her advantage. After turning onto a busy street, she watched Born Ready to see if he would check the back window to make sure Pop was still following. When he did, Queenie went for the pistol, grabbing it by the barrel, trying to snatch it from him.

Born Ready's hand tightened on the butt of the gun like he anticipated the move. And for her lame attempt to disarm him, Born Ready squeezed the trigger, sending a bullet into her rubs.

The Aston Martin's engine revved and the car jerked as she mashed on the gas pedal. A few feet later the luxury car slammed into a Nissan parked at the stop light. Air bags deployed, slapping Queenie and Born Ready in the face.

Dazed and wounded, Queenie limped from the wreck, holding her side, trying to stop the bleeding.

Born Ready shook the stars from his head and noticed the driver's door open. When he seen Queenie limping away, he lifted the 9mm and fired seven times. Three bullets landed in Queenie's back, knocking her to the ground.

The high-pitched sound of an engine made Born Ready look up just in time to see the Maserati slam into the passenger door of the Aston.

Pop Somethin' sprang from the sports car, the 50-caliber hand cannon clutched like an iron sword. He spotted Queenie on the ground, blood pooling around her body. He wanted to go to her, but he had to make sure Born Ready was dead. The last time he didn't finish somebody off, Clutch shot him in the back and he did eight years in prison. So he crept toward the Aston, keeping the 50 ready. The car was mangled, the passenger door folded into Born Ready's body, pinning him in the seat. A snarl was etched on the wounded man's face as blood dripped from his mouth.

Two slugs from the hand cannon tore his face open.

It didn't take Pop long to find the money and go check on Queenie. She lay on the ground, not moving as blood soaked her clothing. "Damn, baby." Pop grieved, squatting down and rolling her over. Queenie moaned in agony, blood covering most of her face. Since the bullets were in her back, Pop knew he couldn't move her for fear of more damage. Confusion spread through him. She was fucked up and needed help right away.

Before he could make up his mind on what to do, sirens sounded in the distance, and thoughts of a prison cell flooded his mind. "I gotta go, baby," Pop groaned, the thought of leaving her making his heart ache.

"No," Queenie moaned weakly, grabbing hold of his pant leg.

"I can't move you. I can't take you wit' me like this."

Tires screeching made Pop look up as Princess sprang from the Batmobile. She ran toward Pop and Queenie, a horrified look on her face. "No, no, no!"

Pop snatched up the bag of money and grabbed Princess around the waist. "We gotta go. Police comin'!"

"No!" Princess fought. "Put her in the car. We can't leave her."

"She fucked up. If we move her, it might make it worse."

Princess continued struggling to get free. "No! I'm not leavin' my sister. Let me go!"

"We can't save her, Princess. We gotta go. She gon' slow us down. The sirens getting' closer."

Princess's fight to get her sister was no match for Pop's strength. He had just shoved her in the Lambo when the first witness showed up, recording with their phone.

***

"We can't just leave her!" Princess screamed, opening the door as the Lamborghini raced away.

Pop reached over and grabbed her arm. "Stop! Ain't shit we can do. She was fucked up. If I woulda moved her, it woulda made it worse. The only chance she got is for them to get her to the hospital. She strong. She gon' be good." When the words left his mouth, Pop knew they were a lie. He had counted at least three bullets in Queenie's back. Her internal organs were shredded. If she didn't die in the streets, she would die on the way to the hospital.

"Damn, Pop," Princes cried, closing the door. "We left her. What if we coulda saved her?"

"She got shot in the back. Her spinal cord mighta got hit. Movin' her woulda made it worse. Ain't no room in here for her, and we can't risk us all gettin' jammed trynna save her. She gon' be good. When she get better, we gon' go get her. For now we gotta get the fuck outta Atlanta and make sure we stay free. Ain't nothin' we can do for her if we get knocked."

Princess sank into the passenger seat as pain and guilt gripped her. She felt like the world had blown up all around her and she was the last person on Earth. The alpha woman who had spent her entire life protecting her was gone. The lioness was no longer roaring.

Pop took his eyes off the road to glance at her. She looked broken. He could feel her pain, and he hoped She wasn't damaged beyond repair.

Instead of going home to grab their already packed bags, Pop hopped on the highway, heading for their new destination. The way he figured; the police were already searching their house because of the shooting. No need to risk their freedom over material shit. He had $200,000 in cash and another $200,000 in a safety deposit box he would probably never see again. The license he used to get the box was at home. But he had more than enough to make a new start. He had done more with less.

After five hours on I-75 and a couple stops to get gas, he pulled into a small hotel in Jacksonville, Florida. He paid the front desk for a room before checking into their sleeping quarters. During the drive, Princess didn't talk much, and that didn't change when they walked in the room.

"You want me to get you somethin'?"

Princess didn't respond right away. She continued to stare up at the ceiling, a spaced out look on her face. "I want my sister."

"Don't do this to yo'self. I know this hard, but you gotta focus on somethin' else."

"I wish we didn't leave her. It's killin' me that I don't know if she still alive." Then she sat up in bed, staring at Pop intently. "You said she was fucked up. How bad? Was she' still talkin'?"

"A li'l bit. It looked like he shot her in the back."

"Be real wit' me, Pop. Do you think she gon' live?"

He paused to think. If he told the truth, that he thought Queenie died in the street, it would probably crush her. If he lied and said Queenie was still alive, it would probably make her feel good, but he didn't like the thought of lying to his bitch. "I really don't know. She strong. And she a fighter."

Princess' face reflected a mix of optimism, pessimism, and exhaustion. "Damn, Pop. I can't stop thinkin' about her. I feel like it's my fault. I just hope she don't...." A painful sob racked her body as the tears began again.

Pop sat next to her, wrapping her in his arms. "It's gon' be okay. I got you. I'ma always be here for you."

After a few minutes of comforting, Princess broke the embrace, staring up at Pop with a deep sadness in her eyes. "I know you don't want me doin' pills, but I need somethin' to take my mind off. I can't stop thinkin' 'bout her. I just need somethin' for tonight. Please."

Pop didn't like the thought of her doing pills again. He had a hard time getting her off them, but it would help her relax. "I'ma go talk to the front desk to see where the strip clubs at. You stayin' here or comin'?"

***

Roxy's was a low-budget strip club in a seedy area of Jacksonville. There were about twenty cars in the parking lot, most of them at least ten years old. Sprinkled in the mix was a couple of donks, but nothing as expensive as the Lambo. The sports car stuck out like the groom wearing a black suit at an all-white wedding. The first thing Pop noticed when they walked in Roxy's was the smell. Vomit, piss, sweat, weed, and liquor. Some of the lights didn't work, so the club was dim. Niki Minaj and Beyonce's "Flawless" played through a stereo system that sounded like it belonged in a '90s basement party. There were no bottle girls, no VIP section, and nobody making it rain. The dancers were average-looking chubby women with stretch marks and scarred bodies that had no business in a thong, let alone a strip club.

"This look like some shit outta one of them old-ass Blaxploitation movies," Pop commented.

"I don't even know what that is, but it sounds bad. We ain't gotta be here long. This a nasty-ass club, and these some nasty-ass bitches," Princess said as she sat at an empty table.

They didn't have to wait long for the entertainment to arrive. A brown-skinned woman who looked every bit of forty-five years old sashayed over. She wore a cheap, lace-front wig, had a wide nose, big lips, and a gap between her front teeth big enough to stick a drum stick through. Her sagging breasts were supported by a bra that was a size too big, and her stomach hung over the front of the purple thong.

She smiled at Pop, reaching out to touch his dreads. "Hey, baby. I'm–"

"Don't touch me!" Pop growled, grabbing her arm.

His aggressive gesture and serious look made the woman shrink back. "O-okay, man. I was just trynna dance for you."

"Don't worry 'bout him," Princess spoke up. "We not lookin' for entertainment. We just wanna get in and out. I need some beans. Any of these niggas in here holdin'?"

The veteran stripper eyed Princess suspiciously. "I don't know what you talkin' 'bout, love. Ain't no drugs in here. We all say no to drugs. I got grand–"

"I got a hunnit dollars if you show me who holdin'," Princess cut her off, holding out a c-note.

The money disappeared into the woman's bra quicker than a magician doing a card trick. "Red Dot over there." She pointed. "I'ma send him over."

Princess looked toward the table the woman pointed at and seen two men and a woman seated. The stripper walked over and said something to a tall, skinny, dark-skinned man who wore tight-fitting designer clothes. He eyed Pop Somethin' as he walked over.

"What hangin', mane? Shawty said y'all trynna power up."

"Yeah," Princess spoke up. "Percs, Xans, or Oxy."

"I got Perc 30s and a couple Xans."

"Gimme those 30s. How many you got?"

"'Bout ten. How many you want?"

"All of 'em. You got a number?"

"She don't need no number," Pop spoke up. "This a one-time."

"C'mon, brah. My shit valid. Straight from the pharmacy. No fuck-shit ova here. Shawty can get my number. I ain't gon' take her from you. This bidness," he laughed, reaching out and touching Pop on the shoulder.

Pop mugged him. "Don't touch me no more. And stop playin' wit' me. You don't know me. Niggas get killed for playin' too much."

Red Dot's face twisted into a snarl, and he spoke out of his thin chest. "Fuck you thank you is, dawg? You in my neck of da woods, boi. We play for keeps 'round here!"

Pop's look changed from serious to seriously irritated. The muscles in his jaw flexed as he tried to keep himself from breaking the young punk in half. "Give up dem pills and move, fuck-boy. I ain't givin' out no more passes."

Instead of using wisdom, Red Dot displayed foolish bravado and reached for his waist. The movement was slow and telegraphed. Pop was less than two feet away. The big man's right hand lashed out like a deadly snake, wrapping around the pill slinger's throat. In the same moment, Pop stood, lifting Red Dot high in the air and choke-slamming him through the table. The 40-caliber pistol he attempted to grab fell on the floor. Pop grabbed it, pressing the barrel to Red Dot's throat.

"Hold on, brah! Hold on!" someone yelled.

Pop looked around and seen a short, brown-skinned man holding his hands up. It was the other man from the table. He had a burn mark on the side of his face and a glass eye in his right eye socket. In his good eye was the fear of God.

"Don't kill 'im, mane. Whatever he said, he ain't mean. That's my li'l cousin. Don't kill 'im."

Pop looked around and seen everyone in the club watching him. Witnesses. If he killed Red Dot, he would have to kill everybody, and he didn't have enough bullets.

Instead of blowing the punk's brains out, Pop dug in his pockets and took the bag of pills. "I should take yo' shit and burn yo' ass, nigga, but I', trynna duck off. I'ma give you five hunnit dollas, and you gon' act like you neva seen us. Respect my gangsta, nigga. And recognize a goon when you see one."

After standing and counting out five hundred dollars, Pop dropped the money on the floor, tucked his new pistol, and headed for the exit. He and Princess were about to hop into the Batmobile when the club door opened. The goon and goonette went for their heats.

"I just wanna talk!" a woman called, holding her hands in the air.

Princess recognized her as the female sitting at the table with Red Dot. She was average height, dark-skinned with a curvy frame. "What you want?"

"I just wanna talk. I think I know you."

Pop gave Princess a look. "Fuck goin' on?"

"I don't know her," Princess said before turning to the woman. "Who is you? How you know me?"

"I got a uncle name Larry. He my daddy, Bruce, brother. Ain't yo' momma name Patricia?"

Princess couldn't hide her surprise. "I remember uncle Bruce Damn, is you April?"

"Nah, that's my sister. I'm Tanya. You one of the twins, right?"

"I hate to break up y'all family reunion," Pop interrupted, "but what up witcho people in there? They ain't strappin' up or callin' twelve, is they?"

Tanya laughed. "Nah, they in there clownin' Red Dot ass. He think he tough, and they was happy to see him get fucked up. Y'all good."

Pop was satisfied with the response, so he nodded to Princess before ducking into the Lambo.

"That nigga betta stop playin', girl. We don't fuck around," Princess said.

"I see. What you doin' in Florida?"

"It's a long story. We might just be passin' through. We don't know yet. You live here?"

"Yeah, not too far from here. I just came here wit' my nigga so he could holla at Red Dot. They cousins."

"Gimme yo' number so we can catch up later. We been on this highway for house, and I need some rest. But I'ma call you when I wake up."

Chapter 2

Pop awoke the next day and found Princess in bed, staring at her phone. "What up? You good?"

"We gotta go back to Atlanta."

Pop looked at her like she was crazy. "What?"

"I just got off the phone with the hospital. Queenie might still be alive. They found two females. One was dead and the other one recovering from surgery. They won't tell me who over the phone. They want me to come identify her."

Pop shook his head. "I'm not goin' back to Atlanta. That's out. And I don't think you should go, either. What driver's license you gon' use? All I got is the Quinten one 'cause I left it in the Lambo. Everything else was in our bags at the old house."

"I left all mine in the house, too. But we gotta see if it's her, Pop. I need to know if my sister still alive."

"I hear you, but you can't go. What if they lookin' for us? You gotta send somebody. What about yo' cousin? We can buy her a plane ticket."

Princess' face lit up as she searched her phone for Tanya's number. "Hey, cousin. This Princess."

"I know. You finally woke up?"

"Yeah. I need to talk to you, and it's important."

"Okay. What's up?"

"Not on the phone. Face to face."

"Um. Ricco at work and I don't got no babysitter. Do you know yo' way around? Don't that fancy car y'all was in got GPS?"

***

All eyes were on the Lamborghini as it pulled to the curb in front of the six-unit apartment complex. The locals called the neighborhood 'The Jungle', and it was no different than every hood in America. Neglected houses, wild shrubbery, balding lawns, and a bunch of outdated cars lined the block. Th. residents in The Jungle didn't see six figure sport cars in their neck of the woods, so the

Lambo got everyone's attention.

Pop stepped from the car wearing a tight-fitting, black Ferragamo t-shirt, black Ferragamo jeans, and shoes. His dreads hung loosely past his shoulders, the fluffy, trimmed beard covering most of his face.

Princess climbed from the passenger seat looking tall and skinny-thick, her red dreadlocks swaying with the switch of her hips. Dressed simply in a corset jumpsuit and Giuseppe heels, she was stunning.

After finding apartment 4, they knocked on the door. "Hey, girl," Tanya answered, carrying a toddler on her hip. The long-lost cousin had Hershey-dark skin, high cheek bones, perfectly-shaped lips, and dangerously seductive brown eyes. She wore a t-shirt and leggings, the stretch pants showing off a body made to lust after. Tanya knew she looked good, but didn't use it to chase a check. She was a simple woman who lived in the hood and struggled with her man like everybody else she knew.

"Hey, cousin!" Princess beamed. "She is so cute. Look just like yo' ass."

"Er'body say that. Y'all come in."

After they had seats on the couch, Princess got right down to business. "I need you to fly to Atlanta to check on my sister. She in the hospital. She got shot. We can't go back 'cause the police might be looking for us."

Surprise showed on Tanya's face. "She got shot? When?"

"Yesterday. The hospital said they got two women victims, but they won't say who is who over the phone. I'll buy you a plane ticket and give you a thousand dollars."

Tanya was lost for words.

The front door opened and Ricco walked into the apartment. He wore a white button-up shirt, black slacks, and Air Force Ones. The wound on the side of his head was fully visible, a burn-like welt going from his eye to the back of his ear. His right eye was also missing, replaced by a prosthetic. When he seen Pop sitting on the couch, his eyes grew wide with surprise. The glass eye threatened to pop out of his face.

"Baby, this my cousin, Princess, and her nigga, Pop Somethin," Tanya introduced.

"What up?" Ricco nodded, keeping it cool.

Pop nodded.

"Hey, Ricco," Princess waved.

"Princess want me to go to Atlanta to check on her sister. She got shot."

Ricco looked from his girl to Princess. "Y'all in some shit? Why you need her to go to Atlanta?"

"We gon' give y'all a thousand dollars and a plane ticket. I don't got ID, and the police might be lookin' for me. I need to know if my sister still alive. I called the hospital, but they won't say over the phone."

Ricco looked unsure "I don't know. Shit don't sound right, and I don't want my girl in no bullshit."

"She gon be good," Princess assured. "We don't got no enemies. I would go, but I ain't trynna fall into no police traps."

"I'ma do it," Tanya said.

"Hold on, baby!" Ricco protested. "You can't make that decision by yo'self. We family."

Tanya turned to her man. "She is family, too. And we need the money. I'm tired of this roachy-ass apartment. We can use the money to move."

"I'ma give y'all twenty-five hunnit," Pop spoke up, going into his pocket and counting out the money. "We want you on the first thing smokin' to Atlanta. Right there and right back."

The couple looked from the money to one another, then Ricco spoke. "When y'all think the next plane leave?"

Pop and Princess laughed at his instant change.

"I ain't go to college or nothin', mane. I ain't even got no GED. I'm a janitor at a car dealership. I can't turn down twenty-five hunnit."

Pop Somethin' appreciated Ricco's realness. Everyone he'd been around as of late was having it, trying to get it, or lying about what they had. "I ain't been around a nigga like you in a long time, brah. Hearin' a nigga trynna get it the right way is rare nowadays."

"The more you got, the more niggas hate. 'More money, more problems' is prolly the realest lyrics I ever heard."

Pop gave the one-eyed mad a long look. The wound told him Ricco had been through something. And quoting the rap lyrics spoke volumes. "What happened to yo' face?"

Ricco looked away, rubbing his facial wound. "A lesson learned the hard way."

Silence engulfed the living room as the words hung in the air. A cry from the baby brought everybody back to the moment.

"What is her name?" Princess asked.

"Yanna. She our li'l angel," Tanya said, kissing the baby atop the head.

"How long y'all gon' be in Florida?" Ricco asked.

"I don't know yet," Pop answered. "We lookin' got a new place to call home. Tell me 'bout Jacksonville. Only thing I know is y'all got a football team."

"First thing I'ma tell you is if you tryna lay low, that Lambo gon' draw more attention than you want. And Jacksonville ain't no different than nowhere else in Florida. Got niggas gettin' a bag and jack-boys trynna take it. The culture is fast. Florida is a tourist state, so you get a lotta people from all over."

"I seen the way er'body was watchin' when I pulled up. These the only wheels I got for now. I don't know my way around. We don' need y'all to show us. Where can I get a rental?"

***

"When you get to the next light, make a right. This the strip. The part of Jacksonville you see in travel brochures. Hotels, beaches, all that kinda shit."

Pop guided the Batmobile through traffic, impressed by the city and the sights. Palm trees, beautiful beaches, and big-ass hotels were all around. "This don't look like a bad spot. What the night life like?"

"I haven't been out in a while. I don't really do much 'cause I'm trynna stay out the way. I'm all about the fam. But you can do anything out here. Strip clubs, concerts, gambling. All that shit."

Pop gave his passenger a look. Why you layin' so low?"

"You ask a lotta questions, mane," Ricco chuckled.

"If you don't know, you gotta ask, right?"

"That's right," he smiled. "Nah, I ain't layin' low. What about you? What happened in Atlanta?"

Pop thought for a moment. "Our season was up."

"What that mean?"

"It's a season for everything. Like a farmer. Sowing and reaping. We sowed and reaped. Now we movin' on."

Ricco gave him a sideways look. "I ain't always been a janitor, my nigga. Quit wit' the riddles. You got my girl getting' in some shit we don't know nothin' about. I ain't no bitch or snitch. We puttin' a lotta trust in y'all. Even though our girls share the same blood, we all still strangers. I appreciate the money, but what's good? Is y'all on the run? Is my girl gon' get in y'all shit if she go to Atlanta?"

Pop looked into Ricco's good eye and seen a street nigga staring back at him, so he told the truth. "Yeah, we on the run from the police. We went to Atlanta to get a bag and shit got ugly on the way out. Queenie got hit up in the process. Y'all don't gotta worry 'bout no niggas gettin' at Tanya in Atlanta 'cause I deaded all that shit. We worried 'bout the police. We don't know what they know. A shootout happened at our house, and we left everything. We had a bunch of fake identities. If Tanya can go check on Queenie and ask a few questions, it would help us out a lot."

"I'ma be real, brah. I don't like the way none of that shit sound. Tanya and my daughter all I got. I can't let nothin' happen to my family."

Pop seen the concern and determination etched across Ricco's face and knew he would do anything to protect his family. "I ain't gon' put yo' family in harm's way. We just need to know if Queenie still alive."

After an intense stare-down, some of the tension left Ricco's body. "The car rental is on the next block. And the storage ain't too far away." After a brief pause, he spoke again. "You should let me drive the Lambo to the storage. I never drove one that was automatic."

Pop gave him a look. "You drove a Lamborghini before?"

"Yeah. A long time ago. But it was a stick."

"I thought you was a workin' nigga that was all about family an' shit. How you drivin' Lambos?"

Ricco gave a sly smile, a gleam showing in his good eye. "It's a lot you don't know about me. I ain't always been no janitor, my nigga."

***

When the plane landed, Tanya could feel the panic rising within. Not only was this her first time on a plane, but it was the first time she'd left the state of Florida in ten years. The potential for unknown danger made her body shiver as she walked off the plane and through the airport. Following the directions from Princess, she hopped a to the hospital.

Sitting behind the information desk was a middle-aged black lady with close-cropped hair wearing pink glasses. Her nametag said Susan.

"Excuse me. I'm looking for my cousin, Taymar Mitchell. She got shot two days ago."

The woman began typing on the keyboard. "Could you spell the name for me?"

"T-a-y-m-a-r M-i-t-c-h-e-l-l."

"I don't see anyone under that name. Does she have an alias?"

"I don't know. She came in with another woman. They said it was a car accident and shooting. I talked to somebody on the phone, and they said I had to come identify her in person."

The woman's face lit up. "Oh, I remember talking to you. The GSW victim came in with the car accident victim two days ago. We didn't' know the shooting victim's name."

"Is she okay?" Tanya asked, feeling hopeful.

"It doesn't say. I'm going to call upstairs and they should be down to talk to you in a moment. Can I get your name?"

"Tanya Manners."

"Okay, Tanya. If you have a seat in the waiting room, someone will come get you."

As soon as Tanya sat down, she called Princess. "Hey, cousin! I'm here, but they told me to wait in the waiting room."

"What happened? Is Queenie still alive?"

"I don't know yet. I'm waitin' for somebody to come talk to me. The receptionist won't say. But she called upstairs. As soon as I know somethin', I'ma call you."

"Okay. Does anything look suspicious? You okay?"

Tanya glanced around to see if anything looked out of the ordinary. "Not that I can tell. But I'm scared as hell, and I don't even know why."

"You good. We don't got no enemies. We just worried about the police."

"Yeah. I know. But I'm still nervous. How is my baby?"

"She's good. Right here watchin' cartoons."

"Okay. I'm about to text Ricco and let him know I landed safely. I'ma call you as soon as I talk to somebody."

After hanging up the phone, she sent her man a text. She was reading his reply when something caught her eye. Two white men wearing dark suits walked into the hospital. They went over to the receptionist and said a few words, then the woman pointed at Tanya. She knew they were the police, and she was in trouble. She thought about running, but her feet wouldn't work. Visions of Yanna and Ricco flashed in her mind.

"Are you Tanya Manners?" the taller man asked.

"Y-yes."

"I'm Detective Renner, and this is my partner. We want to ask you some questions. Can you come with us?"

J-Blunt

Chapter 3

"How long you wanna stay in Jacksonville?"

"Pop looked up from his phone, locking eyes with Princess. She was sitting on the couch with Yanna watching cartoons. "I'm thinkin' we should stay. We can use what Ricco and Tanya know about the city to our advantage. It's better than going somewhere we don't know nobody and trynna establish new relationships. Plus, Tanya already showed she willin' to make moves if the price is right."

"Stay outta my head, nigga," Princess smiled. "I was thinkin' the same shit. Plus, it's somethin' 'bout that nigga, Ricco. He got secrets."

"Understatement. I looked in that nigga good eye and seen somethin'. He told me he drove a Lambo before. It's somethin' to this nigga, and I think he might be the key to us turnin' up."

"So, what we gon' do wit' the money we left in Atlanta? Do we leave it and use what we got to get started?"

I don't think we got a choice. I left the license that I used to get that safety deposit box back at the house. Twelve got that. But I still got the key."

"Can't we just get another license in that name? We can't just leave all that money and not try to find it."

"I'ma try to go back and get it. Trust me. But for now, we gotta use what we got. I think this more than enough to put us on. We just find the right niggas to help us flip this shit. And get a plug."

"So, we back to Ricco."

Pop Something nodded. "Back to Ricco. And Tanya, too. She still ain't called back yet?"

Princess checked her phone. "Nah. Somethin' don't seem right. She shoulda texted me back by now. It's been over an hour."

"I don't like that shit. Damn."

The phone started ringing in her hand. "This her!" Princess screamed, answering the phone on speaker. "Girl, where you been? You okay?"

"I just left the police station. I'm on my way to the airport. "

"The police station?" Pop and Princess said simultaneously.

"Yeah. They questioned me about Queenie. I think she still alive."

"My sister alive?" Princess screamed.

"Yeah. I think. But she missing."

Some of the excitement in Princess' voice vanished. "What? She missin'? How?"

"They don't know. The doctors did surgery as soon as she got to the hospital and she was bein' guarded 'cause the police wanted to talk to her when she woke up. They had security outside her door. But somehow she missin'."

Princess was stunned and unable to speak.

"Did they say anything about us or how she got shot?" Pop asked.

"Yeah. They showed pictures of you and Princess. They didn't say y'all did anything, but they wanna talk. I told 'em I didn't know you, but I don't think they believed me."

"Damn!" Pop cursed. "A'ight. Good lookin' for doin' this for us. Come back home."

After hanging up the phone, Princess stared over at Pop. "I gotta find my sister."

"You heard what Tanya said. Twelve lookin' for us. We can't go back to Atlanta."

Princess stood and began pacing the living room. "But she still alive! What if somebody kidnapped her? We don't know nobody in Atlanta that would try to help her. Ain't nobody called us. She might be in trouble."

"We can't go back to Atlanta," Pop repeated, finality in his voice. "If we get locked up, we won't be able to help her at all. Only thing we can do is sit back and wait 'til we hear somethin' or she get at us. Let's just focus on her bein' alive. That's good news."

Princess flopped down on the couch, letting out a deep sigh. "Damn, Pop. This don't make sense. I want my sister."

"We gon' get to the bottom of this. That's my word. But right now we gotta focus on the shit we can control. Like seein' if we can getcho cousin and Ricco to join the team."

***

The revving of the twin turbo engine made the people standing outside Pole Boulevard look toward the parking lot. The black Lamborghini coasted through the lot, getting admiring stares from the strip club patrons. Pop and Princess stepped from the sleek automobile with the air of Jay-Z and Beyoncé, both dressed in Valentino. The newest Jacksonville residents soaked up the spotlight as they walked toward the club entrance.

After parking Pop Somethin's rented Lexus CUV behind the Batmobile, Ricco and his girl followed Pop and Princess, enjoying the envious looks they got from the people standing in line. Ricco was dressed simply in a pair of jeans and a blazer. Tanya stole the show, wearing a white Marc Jacobs dress. Standing five-five with dark skin and crazy curves, the skin-tight white dress made her body look like it had been molded by the hands of God.

After stopping to have a brief conversation with security, the foursome was allowed into the club. To be in Pole Boulevard on opening night was something special. To be in Pole Boulevard's VIP on the grand opening was extraordinary.

The club was owned and operated by Kevin 'KV' Childress, a big time drug-dealer-turned-business-man from Miami. Everybody who was somebody was in Pole Boulevard. Rappers, singers, movie stars, athletes, and Pop, Princess, Tanya, and Ricco.

"Oh my God! This feels so unreal!" Tanya fangirled out, looking around the club in awe. "Is that Block Boy? I know all his songs!"

"Chill, baby. Don't fan out. We gotta act like we been in places like this before," Ricco said coolly, adjusting his Prada shades.

"But I never been in a place like this before. I don't know how I should act," Tanya admitted. "Is that Simone Renae? Can I ask for a selfie?"

"Not right now. We gon' be here awhile. Let's find our booth first. We gon' have time to meet and party wit' er'body."

When they found their booth, a fine and thick bottle girl

approached. "Hey! Welcome to Pole Boulevard. I'm Bunny. Can I get y'all some drinks?"

"I'm good," Pop answered. "What y'all want to drink? It's on me."

"I don't drink," Ricco said.

"Just give us two bottle of Vanilla Ciroc," Princess said.

Pop gave the bottle girl more than enough money to pay for the drinks and a nice tip. When the strippers came over and the drinks began flowing, a good time was had by all.

An hour later the women retreated to the rest room. "Damn, cousin. It feels good gettin' dressed up and goin' out wit' y'all. To be in VIP in here is some baller shit. How y'all do it?" Tanya asked as she stood at the sink, washing her hands.

"Pop did this. We just got to the city, so we don't know nothin' 'bout the hot spots. Ricco prolly told him 'bout it."

"My mystery man, huh?" Tanya commented.

"What happened to his eye?" Princess asked.

"He won't talk about it. I used to ask him about it a lot when we first met. He never told me, so I just learned to live with him and his secrets. It's been two years now."

"Speaking of secrets, I need a favor. You can't tell nobody. Not Ricco, and especially not Pop Somethin'."

Tanya looked anxious to know. "What is it?"

"Chill, gurl. It ain't that serious. I need Red Dot number. I need some pills, and I don't want nobody to know about it."

"Okay. I'ma text him right now."

While Tanya texted, Princess checked her dreads and clothes in the mirror. "Damn, cousin. You wearin' the fuck outta that Marc Jacobs."

"I feel like a model wearin' this shit," Tanya blushed. "I feel good. And pretty. I don't know how I'ma pay you the five hundred dollars for this."

"Don't even worry about it. We told y'all er'thang on us. And we thinkin' 'bout stayin', so it might get better."

That got Tanya's attention. "Y'all stayin'?"

"We thinkin' 'bout it. We really don't got nowhere else to go.

Plus, you here. But we need to make a new plug, so that's kinda weighin' on us."

"What you mean, 'a new plug'?"

Princess met her cousin's stare. "Tanya, we get money. Not little shit. Hundred thousands. We thinkin' 'bout settin' up shop here. And to do that we need people that know they way around. And a dope plug. If you and Ricco help us, y'all can live like this er' night."

The gleam in Tanya's eyes told that she was ready and willing. "I'ma talk to Ricco 'bout it. I'm tired of struggling. If y'all can give away money just to have a good time, we need to hook up."

***

"How long y'all gon' be in Jacksonville?" Ricco asked as he and Pop watched the Puerto Rican stripper put on a show.

"We thinkin' 'bout stayin'. So far I'm likin' the city's vibe."

"Yeah. It's always crackin' 'round here. Shit, all over Florida, really. I thought about movin' to a new state a few years ago, but I couldn't leave the Sunshine State."

Pop threw a few dollars at the stripper. "Yeah, I'm feelin' the same way. You been in Jacksonville all yo' life?"

"Nah. I grew up in Miami. I came here a couple years ago. Met Tanya and made a family."

"What made you leave Miami?"

Ricco gave Pop Somethin' a look. "Why you so interested in me? You ask a lotta questions."

Pop leaned forward. "I'ma keep it a hunnit witchu, brah. It's somethin' 'bout you that got me wantin' to fuck witchu the long way. You got a street' nigga vibe, and I relate to that shit. I see you nine-to-fivin', and I know that shit a front. I peeped how you movin' in here tonight. You used to this. These niggas wit' money don't impress you. You rubbed shoulders wit' these kinda niggas before. You drove Lambos. I see you, brah."

Ricco was silent for a moment, but the look in his eye told the truth. "What you on, brah? You blew a bag on me and my lady. I know this ain't y'all just showin' us a good time. You ain't the only one that can see past what's in front of you. I see you, too."

"I see a street nigga in you, and I respect yo' slot," Pop acknowledged. "I'm trynna get a bag, my nigga. Like the one Santa Claus carry the toys in. But my shit gon' be filled wit' blue cheese. You know the ins and outs of the city. I need to know what you know. I get money, my dude. Let's get to it and getcho family out them ratchet-ass apartments. Upgrade that Ford Fusion into somethin' foreign."

A tormented look shown on Ricco's face, like his soul was being pulled in two directions. "I'm done wit' that life. It cost too much."

Pop studied his face, seeing the internal struggle. "Yo' mouth say one thing, but the look on yo' face say somethin' else. You tired of cleanin' toilets. You want this shit back. Whatever happened in Miami was fucked up, but that's life. Good and bad. Sunshine and rain. You gon' encounter defeats, but you can't let that shit beat you. Get back on the bike and ride that bitch 'til the wheels fall off."

Ricco let out a chuckle. "You shoulda been a motivational speaker, my nigga. That spiel was good, but I'ma pass. Here come my lady. I don't want her to know what we was talkin' 'bout, so let's change lanes. My Jacksonville Jaguars goin' to the Super Bowl this year."

***

"Damn, Pop, I can't feel my legs." Princess laughed as she held onto Pop Somethin's arm.

"In the mornin' we gon' see how much of yo' body you feel when that hangover kick in. I think you outdid yo'self. You and Tanya," he said, looking at Ricco helping Tanya into the rented Lexus.

"That's my bitch! She a bad bitch and don't even know it. And she know how to turn up! Turn up! Turn up! Turn up!" Princess yelled, losing her balance.

Pop grabbed his lady roughly to stop her from falling. "C'mon, girl! Chill 'fore you bust yo' shit."

"Oh! I love when you get aggressive! Come fuck me on the hood of the Lambo so er'body can see."

"Stop playin' and get in the car."

Princess dropped to her knees. "Pull out yo' dick. I wanna suck it right now."

Pop got irritated. "Quit playin' and getcho—"

"Pop, look out!" Ricco called, panic in his voice.

The big man spun around just in time to see two niggas in dark clothes running toward him holding automatic weapons. The 50 was locked in the Lambo, and because of Princess' drunken antics he never got the chance to unlock the door. All he could do was watch as pistols were pointed at his chest.

"Gimme dem keys, nigga!" the lead jacker yelled.

"Fuck!" Pop cursed, pissed off that he had been caught slipping.

When Princess realized what was going on, she stood to face the jackers. "Fuck y'all doin'?" Y'all know who we is? Move around 'fore we fuck y'all up!"

While Princess talked shit, Pop studied the jack boys, noticing the distance they kept from him. He also noticed their serious demeanor. These boys were about their business, and Princess' mouth might get them killed. "Chill, baby. This ain't the time."

Instead of heeding her man's words, Princess went harder. "Nah, fuck that! These niggas ain't shit. We ain't givin'—"

The second jacker moved quickly, pistol-whipping Princess across the head. Pop felt her pain as she went down, thoughts of losing her flashing in his mind. He couldn't lose both his bitches. He had to do something.

"Don't even thank 'bout it, fuck-boy!" the lead jacker spoke up. "Don't turn this to no murda scene. Give up dem keys and walk away."

Pop loved the Lambo, but it wasn't worth dying for, so he went in his pocket for the keys.

"C'mon, mane! Y'all ain't gotta do that," Ricco called.

Both jackers spun at the sound of Ricco's voice. Pop seized the momentary distraction and shoved Princess into the nearest jacker as she was stumbling to her feet. The collision made both of them fall. Pop closed the distance between him and the lead jacker, his fist a blur as it raced toward the distracted man's face.

There was a bone-shattering crunch as the big man's fist met the jacker's jaw. Like a puppet that had its strings clipped, down went the jacker. Without missing a beat, Pop went for jack boy number two as he stumbled to his feet, attempting to point the pistol. Anger, adrenaline, and the fear of being shot propelled Pop into the jacker before he could take aim.

Pow! The gun fired as he crashed into the smaller man, knocking him to the ground. The predator became prey when Pop dove on top of the stunned jacker and took his pistol. A bullet through the nose ended the life of Pop Somethin's first Florida victim.

Knowing the gunshots had alerted others nearby, Pop grabbed Princess and moved toward the Batmobile. He had just unlocked the door and thrown her in the passenger sear when an engine revving got his attention. The jacker with the broken jaw had gotten to his feet and was lifting the pistol. Pop knew he wouldn't be able to lift the pistol in his hand to shoot back or duck before the jack boy shot him.

And he didn't have to. The Lexus CUV raced toward the jacker, smacking him and sending him flying into the air. Pop didn't even wait for his body to hit the ground before he turned and jumped into the Lamborghini.

"My head hurt," Princess whined from the passenger seat.

Pop shot her a mean glance. "You gon' have to find another way to deal wit' losin' Queenie. You ain't finna be sloppy drunk like this no more. You almost got us fucked up."

Princess got an attitude. "What? It ain't my fault they tried to rob us. Don't blame that on me."

"It is yo' fault. I was too busy trynna getcho drunk ass in the car when they crept up. Ain't no way that shoulda happened. All this drinkin' and poppin' pills finna stop. I need you on point. I need you focused."

"Nigga, you can't tell me what to do or how to live my life. You don't know how it feel to lose yo' sister."

"Just because Queenie missin' and it's fuckin' witchu don't mean you can talk to me like that. I'm still yo' nigga."

Princess rolled her eyes, crossing her arms over her chest. "Whatever, nigga."

The drive back to the hotel was silent. When he parked the Lambo, Ricco approached with wide eyes. "We gotta get the fuck outta Jacksonville! Them was J-West niggas. The police gon' be lookin' for us, too. Did you kill him?"

"Chill, brah. I got this," Pop said, trying to calm him. "The rental and Lambo in my name. This ain't gon' get back to you. Take Tanya home. We gon' worry 'bout the rest tomorrow."

"Pop, I don't think you heard me, brah. Them was J-West's niggas! Them niggas deadlier than cancer. You should leave, mane. Right now."

"Nah, I don't think you heard me. Go home. Fuck J-West and his niggas. Them pussy-niggas shouldn'ta tried me. Now they know. Take yo' girl home. I got this."

Ricco looked like he wanted to say more, but instead gave Pop Somethin' a sympathetic look, like he knew it would be the last time they saw one another. Then he turned and helped his girl from the Lexus before hopping in their Ford Fusion and driving away.

Inside the hotel room, Pop sat on the bed, fuming with anger. His plans to set up shop seemed doomed before they could start, and he was putting most of the blame on Princess. Her drunkenness caused him to slip, and he had to body a jacker. And not just any jacker, but one of J-West's niggas, whoever that was. He needed to get rid of the Lambo, but Princess was too drunk to tail him to the storage in the Lexus. He would have to lay low for the night and make the moves after she sobered up.

"Don't be mad, baby," Princess said, crawling up behind Pop and hugging him around the neck.

He removed her arms roughly. "Move."

She wrapped her arms around him again, kissing him on the

neck. "I said I'm sorry. I know I fucked up, but we still alive. Don't be mad."

He stood aggressively, turning around to glare at her. "Sorry ain't enough, Princess. This high stakes! Twelve lookin' for us in Atlanta, and ain't no tellin' who else. We gotta be one step ahead of er'body. Queenie missin' ain't no coincidence. All this shit connected, and we can't afford to get drunk and fuck off. That shit can get us in a cell or grave. All our moves gotta be calculated. We gotta stay focused. And if you sad, depressed, and fuck up on pills and liquor, you ain't gon' be good to nobody."

Princess knelt on the bed, head down, shoulders sagging. Even though she was drunk and high, Pop's words penetrated the fog. Guilt, sadness, and regret flooded her body, bringing on tears. "I'm sorry, baby. I–"

"Stop sayin' sorry!" Pop exploded. "Fuck that sorry shit. What's done is done, and bein' sorry won't change shit. Do better. That's it."

Princess wiped away the tears, squaring up her shoulders. "Okay. I'ma do better. I am. I just feel like a part of me is missin' without my sister. It feels like I'm goin' crazy. I don't know how to handle this."

Pop could see the uncertainty of Queenie's whereabouts eating at Princess. Losing her sister was the worst thing that could've happened, and it was threatening to undo her. She was using the drugs and alcohol to cope. Self-medicating. But he couldn't have her fucked up all the time. That could be detrimental to both of them.

"I feel yo' pain," he whispered, sitting on the bed and wrapping an arm around her shoulder. "I miss her, too. We gon' get her back. That's my word. I need her as bad as you do."

Princess' body molded into Pop's as the murderous duo locked in an embrace. Her tears soaked through his shirt as he held her, and he could feel something stirring within him. Like her pain was being transferred to him. He could feel the connection shared by the sisters, and the pain of the loss threatened to unravel Princess. It was like losing a hand or foot.

Then his own memories of Queenie began to play in his mind. How they met. Her trial by fire. The look on her face when she was lyin' in the streets, bleeding.

Then his feelings and emotions became jumbled and mixed, confusing him. And in the next moment it all made sense. Everything he'd experienced had connected him to Princess on a deeper level. He needed her just like she needed Queenie. She was his lioness. His loyal ride-or-die bitch. She belonged to him. She was his.

Princess broke the embrace to look at Pop. In his eyes she seen her reflection. Then she remembered when they first connected in Texas. When she first became his bitch. "Namaste," she whispered.

Pop leaned close until their foreheads were touching. "I see you, too."

When their lips met, it was nothing like Pop Somethin' had ever felt. A jolt of electricity moved from his tongue to his brain, down his spinal cord, and through his entire body. Princess moaned as similar sensations moved through her body, tingling every nerve ending.

When they fell on the bed, clothes began flying all over the room. After they were naked, Pop climbed between her legs, his mouth finding hers as his tool slipped into her wetness. Instead of playing sex games, Pop controlled himself, taking his time. His strokes were slow and meaningful. Princess responded in kind, giving Pop everything she had to offer. Every thrust was matched by the other partner as they moved in perfect rhythm, in tune with one another's bodies.

When Pop rolled onto his back, Princess never missed a beat as she rode him. She felt so connected to him that she could feel every breath he took. She could smell him, taste him, and feel him at the same time. The pleasure was so intense it brought tears to her eyes as the orgasm began building. And since they were in sync, Pop felt everything she did and releasing his seed into her as they came. Passionate kisses were exchanged as they held one another.

"I need you," Princess whispered in his ear.

"I got you, baby," Pop breathed.

"I'm serious, Pop. I need you. You the only one that can fill the hole she left."

Pop thought about what she was saying. The woman he met back in Texas didn't need anyone. She was strong-willed and independent, but now that Queenie was gone, she was missing a piece. He was the only one who could fill the hole.

She loved him.

"I'm here. I got you."

The lovers became silent as they thought about what they had just shared. They were linked. Feelings were involved.

"I don't wanna be yo' bitch no more, Pop. I wanna be all yours. And I want you to be all mine."

Chapter 4

The small cry from Yanna cut through Ricco's restless slumber as the one-year-old lay next to her father, appearing to be sleep. But he knew her whimpers were a sign of more to come.

Next to the toddler was her mother. Tanya lay on he stomach, mouth open in a drunken sleep. Last night she looked like a model. She was fine and sexy, but never dressed up or played on her looks. She was a humble beauty, and he liked that about her. But seeing her flexing in the designer dress was a sight to see. He wished he could spoil her the way Pop and Princess had. It felt nostalgic, rubbing shoulders with the "Who's Who" of Florida. Visions of life in the fast lane began playing in his mind. Cars, money, women, and jewelry. He wanted it back. He missed the game like a long-lost lover missed their soul mate.

Then he remembered the bullet to the face. The streets brought too many problems. Just like it had last night. He had to run a man over. The fact he injured someone didn't weight that heavy on his mind. He was more concerned about the repercussions. J-West wasn't going to let the death and injury of his boys go unpunished. And then there was the police. Somebody had seen something. There was always a witness.

Kicking it with Pop Somethin' and Princess had proved costly. He just hoped the consequences wouldn't be too severe.

Another cry from Yanna pulled Ricco from his thoughts. The one-year-old was fully awake and demanded her father's attention.

"Hey, baby girl. Why you cryin'?" Ricco asked as he checked her diaper. The mushy pamper confirmed the cause of her cries.

After a wipe and diaper change, Ricco picked up his baby and took her to the kitchen to make a bottle. When he turned on the lights, roaches scattered like niggas on the block being chased by the police. The sight of the pests repulsed him. His daughter and wifey deserved better, but he was an uneducated janitor at a car dealership.

"I'ma get us outta here," he promised Yanna.

The baby sucked the bottle hungrily, staring up at her father with wide, trusting eyes.

***

"What it do?" Ricco greeted Red Dot after letting him in the apartment.

"Just out here trynna get to it," the nappy-headed man smiled, showing off his gold grill. "Is Tanya here?"

"Yeah. She in the back. What you want wit' my girl?"

Red Dot smiled lustfully. "She been hittin' my line lately. She ready to get out these apartments and boss up wit' a real nigga. She chose up, cuz."

Ricco put up his fists and threw a couple jabs. "You trynna die early, young nigga?"

"I'm fuckin' witchu!" Red Dot laughed. "She hit me last night 'bout some percs, and I told her I was gon' come through today. I don't want yo' bitch. She bad, but she ain't thotty enough for me."

"Don't be callin' my girl no bitch, nigga. And what you mean she hit you for some pills?"

"Ask her, nigga. I just want the money."

"Tanya!"

"What?" she called from the back of the apartment.

"Bring yo' ass here!"

A few moments later Tanya walked in the living room carrying Yanna on her hip. "What's wrong? Why you callin' me like that?"

"Fuck Red Dot talkin' 'bout you buyin' pills?"

She mugged the pill peddler. "Damn, nigga. I told you not to say nothin'."

Red Dot shrugged nonchalantly. "My bad. I forgot."

Ricco felt his body grow warm as jealousy filled him. "Fuck y'all keepin' secrets for?"

"Chill, baby. It ain't even like that."

"Kinda shit y'all on? I know you muthafuckas ain't trynna play me! I swear to God–"

"I told you it ain't like that. Don't nobody want yo' cousin. Ugh!" Tanya said, frowning at Red Dot before turning back to her man. "Can't neither one of y'all say nothin'."

"Say nothin' 'bout what?" Ricco asked, anxious to know.

Tanya took a breath. "They for my cousin. She don't want Pop Somethin' to find out, so I got 'em for her."

Ricco gave her a long stare. "I ain't feelin' these secrets or you buyin' dope for her."

"It ain't nothin' but some pills, baby. Relax. All the undercover shit you and Red Dot be doin', you shouldn't talk. Where you go last weekend when you wasn't answerin' yo' phone? You wanna start some shit, we can do it."

Ricco calmed, not wanting to get into his secrets. "Whatever, man. We ain't finna go there. I told you my phone died. Get the damn pills."

"I know, nigga," Tanya smiled before turning to mug Red Dot. "Gimme some percs, snitch."

"I ain't no snitch, bird. What you want?"

"Whatever I can get for two-fifty. I'ma go grab the money."

When Tanya walked away, Red Dot watched her ass jiggle in the stretch pants. "Damn, cuz! You know shawty a gold mine, right? Put her ass in Pole Boulevard and y'all be in a mansion in six months."

"What I tell you 'bout lookin' at my girl ass?" Ricco flexed.

"Get out cho feelins, sucka-ass nigga. Ain't nothin' wrong wit' lookin'. I don't want yo' girl. I told you, I like mine heavy on the slutty side."

"Whatever, nigga. Speakin' of Pole, did you hear 'bout what happened last night?"

"Did I? Streets ain't stopped talkin' 'bout that shit. J-West cousin got whacked, and the otha nigga in ICU. That's what them fuck-niggas get. That jack-shit is some fuck-shit. Niggas ain't got no grind, so they get on that bullshit. I'm glad them niggas got they issue."

"I was there," Ricco said somberly. "I seen that shit."

Red Dot looked like he took a hit off a crack pipe. "On what? You was at Pole last night? How the fuck you get in? What happened?"

Ricco shook his head like he was trying to erase a bad memory. "We went wit' Princess and Pop Somethin'. They tried to take his Lambo, and he fucked them niggas up. Nigga was on some action hero, Navy Seal-type shit. I ain't neva seen a nigga put in work like that. He savage."

Red Dot's hand move unconsciously to his throat as he relived being choke-slammed through the table. "Damn. Who the fuck is this nigga? You think he was in the Army?"

"I don't know. I think he a street nigga, but he a beast. He wanna set up shop in Jacksonville and want me on the team. I think he got a bag, too."

Red Dot got excited. "When we gettin' to it? I ready to eat, for real!"

"I ain't fuckin' wit' that nigga. He got niggas and twelve lookin' for him all over the United States. They on the run from Atlanta. And after last night, I know why. I had to run one of them niggas over."

Red Dot looked ready to explode. "You trippin', nigga! Fuck them bitch-ass niggas. And this ain't Miami. You got the chance for a new start. Ball on they ass again. How you go from bein' That Nigga to bein' that nigga at a car lot cleanin' bathrooms? This yo' shot, nigga. Let's get to it."

"Get to what?" Tanya asked, walking into the living room.

"Nothin'," Ricco said. "Why you creepin' up like that?"

She handed the money to Red Dot. "I wasn't. Y'all talkin' loud. Now, what y'all gettin' to?"

"Shit. We was talkin' 'bout Pole Boulevard."

Tanya smiled. "I had fun, baby. I was so fucked up that I don't remember how the night ended. Shit, I don't even remember comin' home. I didn't do nothin' stupid, did I?"

"Nah. You was good, baby. I kept an eye on you."

"Good. Princess comin' over later. I'ma go out wit' her. They lookin' for a house, and she want my help."

***

"You was turnt last night!" Princess laughed. "You was clappin' ass and grabbin' titties like you wanted to take one of them bitches home wit' y'all."

"I'm surprised I'm able to move around. I was so fucked up that I don't remember shit."

Princess swallowed one of the percs and chased it with a shot of Hennessy. "You don't remember what happened when we was leavin'?"

Tanya took her eyes off the road to look at her cousin. "Don't tell me I did some stupid shit? I asked Ricco, and he said I was good."

"You really don't remember?" Princess asked again.

"Nah. I told you I was fucked up."

"Some niggas tried to rob us. Pop Somethin' shot one, and Ricco ran the other one over."

"Stop playin'," Tanya laughed. "That ain't funny."

"I ain't playin'. I'm serious. Pop Somethin' killed a nigga. I think Ricco killed the other one."

Shock and awe shown on Tanya's face. "I don't remember none of that. Where was I at?"

"In the car wit' Ricco. We was in the parking lot."

When the reality of it all dawned on Tanya, she panicked. "Oh shit! They really killed people? Who was it?"

"We not sure. Pop mentioned a nigga named J-West."

Tanya's eyes popped. "He killed J-West?"

"Nah. They was his niggas. Who is J-West?"

Tanya looked visibly shaken. "Somebody y'all shouldn'ta fucked wit'. Him and his niggas don't play. Er'body in the city get spooked when they come around. Did they see y'all faces? Do they know who we is?"

"I don't know, but we need to find out. Do you know anybody that know them niggas?"

Tanya paused. "Um. Not really."

Princess noticed the hesitation. "What that mean? Yes or no? Don't bullshit right now. This shit serious."

"I do, but I don't. This bitch I used to know used to fuck one of them niggas. But Ricco don't want me talkin' to her."

"Well, Ricco ain't here. I need you to find her so we can find this nigga. We need to know if they lookin' for us."

"I thought you wanted to go look for a house?"

"The house can wait. We gotta make sure we be alive long enough to pay the rent. Call her."

"Right now?" Tanya asked.

"Nah, bitch. Yesterday."

"I don't got her number. But I can prolly find her on Facebook."

"Do it. Matter fact, gimme yo' phone. I'll do it."

"When I talk to her, what I'm s'posed to say? I ain't talked to her in damn near a year."

Princess thought fast. "Has she seen Yanna?"

Tanya looked spooked. "I don't want her in this."

"I don't think you understand what's on the line. If J-West and his niggas is who you say they is, we gotta move fast. Time and information is everything. We can't just sit back and wait for them niggas to decide what they gon' do to us. That's how we end up dead, and you won't have to worry 'bout puttin' yo' daughter in this. I know what I'm doin'. Trust me. Call yo' friend and tell her you miss her. We can handle the rest later."

***

Star was the definition of a thotty ho bitch, and calling her that to her face wasn't disrespectful. In fact, she embraced it, loving her reputation as a money-hungry freak. Standing five-five with curves crazier than a figure eight, the dark-skinned stripper knew how to use what she had to get what she wanted.

"Damn. She is so fuckin' cute. I can't believe you waited this long to let me see her. I'm mad at you for this, bitch," Star said resentfully as she bounced Yanna on her lap.

"Gurl, you know Ricco hate yo' ass. I gotta live wit' this nigga, and I was tired of hearin' y'all talk shit to each other and about each other."

Star cut her eyes at Tanya. "So, that mean you choose yo' nigga over yo' bitch? You know how it go. Hos over bros."

"She got a point," Princess cut in.

Tanya eyed her cousin. "Really?"

"I'm just sayin', we gotta stick to the ho code how niggas stick to they bro code."

Star laughed loudly, slapping Princess a high five. "Now this is my type of bitch! Keep that shit real, cousin. What you say yo' name was again?"

"Princess."

"Yeah, Princess. Tell her ass the truth. That's the problem wit' bitches nowadays. We keep turnin' on each other for these no-good, li'l dick-ass niggas. Where all the real bitches at?"

"Right here, bitch," Tanya said. "My daughter need her father, and he ain't got no li'l dick. You need to be worried about yo' nigga. Where Derion li'l dick-ass at?"

"Gurl, Derion bitch-ass is old news. His punk-ass gon' fuck Tasty nasty-ass. I cut him and that bitch off. They can have each other."

"Yo, cousin. Tasty?" Tanya laughed. "She did that?"

"Yeah. You know her nasty-ass don't give a fuck who she fuck. These hos ain't loyal. Just 'cause we share the same blood don't mean shit. The muthafuckas you share blood wit' will fuck you over the fastest. That's why I don't fuck wit' these bitches. I'm all about my coins. If a muthafucka ain't eatin' this pussy or puttin' some money in my bag, fuck 'im."

"Talk that shit, bitch," Princess sang. "I been waitin' to meet a bitch like you, Star. Tanya prissy-ass too stuck up. Chase a check. Neva chase a dick!"

"Hey! That's what I'm talkin' 'bout!" Star bounced, doing a shimmy-shake.

Tanya shook her head. "Y'all way too much."

"See, that's that prissy-ass shit yo' cousin was talkin' 'bout. Bitch, you need to come put on some heels and come shake some ass wit' me at the titty club. Yanna gave you some ass and hips. You need to use what God gave you to get y'all ass out them projects."

Tanya gave a funny look. "Bitch, I don't gotta shake my ass to get out the projects. Ricco is my man, and he got it. Soon as he get the salesman job, we gon' be good. As long as I got him and my baby, we gon' be okay."

Star imitated throwing up.

"What club you at?" Princess asked.

"Safari. A li'l strip club downtown. It's poppin' on the weekends. You know somethin' 'bout the nightlife?"

"Girl, if it's 'bout money, I'm there. When they do tryouts?"

"Shit, I know the manager. Lucky keep his tongue up my ass. Since you my girl cousin, I'ma put you in. Gimme yo' number before y'all leave."

"I will. So, who is this nigga, Derion? I think I know him."

"You prolly do. He a ho-ass nigga that run wit' a group of ho-ass niggas. Call theyself Goon Squad. J-West is they daddy. Whatever he say, they do."

"Yeah. That's his bitch-ass. You know if he was at Pole Boulevard last night?"

Star cut her eyes at Princess. "Damn, bitch. You ask a lotta questions. What you on?"

Princess gave a sly smile. "Was I that obvious?"

Star looked from Princess to Tanya. "What yo' cousin on?"

"We was at Pole last night."

"Did you hear what happened?" Princess asked.

"I still don't know why you hos askin' me all these questions. Lemme find out one-a you bitches wearin' a wire and I'ma fuck y'all up."

"Bitch, please!" Tanya frowned.

"Ain't nobody the police," Princess said. "We had a run wit' Goon Squad last night. You heard anything?"

Star looked amused. "That was y'all that fucked up Laro and Queezy?"

Princess nodded. "They tried to rob us."

"Damn. The whole city talkin' 'bout that shit. Laro in the hospital about to die, and Queezy dead. But y'all already know."

"What the streets sayin'? Do they know who we is?"

"Nah, I don't think so. But I'm not sure. I heard this through the grapevine, and you know how shit get twisted."

"Can you get in touch wit' Derion to find out for sure? We payin'."

Star smiled. "Bitch, you shoulda led wit' that. I told you hos I ain't loyal to nothin' but my coins. I need my car note paid. What you want me to do?"

A loud knock on the door stopped Princess from answering.

"Who the fuck knockin' on my muthafuckin' door like this?" Star questioned as she handed Tanya her baby and stormed toward the door. "Who is it?"

"Where that punk-bitch Star at?" a woman screamed from outside. "You thought I wouldn't find out where you lived, ho? Come outside and say that shit to my face!"

Star looked through the peephole and seen three women standing on her porch. "I don't know who y'all bitches think y'all fuckin' wit', but y'all betta get off my muthafuckin' porch!"

The women began beating on the door, un-phased by the threat. "This Bridget, bitch. You talked that shit on Facebook, now say it to my face."

Princess pulled the 40-caliber Pop took from Red Dot out of her purse.

"Where you get that?" Tanya asked. "What you about to do?"

"I don't leave the house without it. And if them bitches don't leave, I'ma put some holes in they ass." Then she turned to Star. "Who is Bridget?"

"Some hatin'-ass bitch who nigga been cashin' me out. She found my pictures in his phone and started trollin' me. Lemme go get my shit. I'ma show these hos," Star said before ducking into her bedroom. She came out a few moments later holding a 9mm with a pearl handle. "I told these bitches to get the fuck off my porch."

After unlocking the door, Star charged outside, her pistol high. *Clap. clap. clap. clap!* She fired in the air. The women stumbled and tripped over one another as they ran off the porch. Instead of letting them go. Star chased them, swinging her pistol and slapping them upside the heads. Princess stood in the doorway smiling, loving the way Star took care of business. Tanya stood next to her cousin, watching the show with wide eyes.

"Don't come by my house talkin' that shit no more, you punk-ass bitches," Star screamed at the terrified women as they hopped in a red Chevy Impala. "And tell yo' li'l-dick-ass nigga to lose my number!"

"Yo' girl crazy," Princess laughed.

Tanya shook her head. "I know."

Chapter 5

A loud knock on the door broke Red Dot's concentration on 2K20. "Damn. They knockin' like they the police."

"Hold on. Lemme get that," Ricco said, pausing the game. "Who is it?"

"Pop Somethin'."

The cousins gave each other wide-eyed looks. "Fuck he want?" Red Dot whispered.

Ricco shrugged.

"Think he know 'bout the pills?"

Ricco shrugged again. "I don't know. But don't say shit. I got it." After opening the door, he greeted the big man coolly. "What's good, brah? Princess gone."

"I know. I need to holla at you," Pop said flatly.

"A'ight. Come in."

Red Dot acknowledged Pop Somethin' with a nod when he walked into the apartment. The goon stone-faced him as he sat on the couch.

"What up, Pop?" Ricco asked, anxious to know what he wanted.

"First, good lookin' for comin' through for me at the club. That nigga had the ups on me, and you took care of that. That was real shit."

"It wasn't shit, fam. You been showin' me and wifey a lotta love since you been here. I was just returnin' the favor. Favor for a favor, my nigga."

Pop mugged him, showing open hostility. "Don't say that shit no more."

Ricco looked puzzled. "What you talkin' 'bout? What I do?"

"I blazed the last two niggas that told me that shit."

The living room grew quiet as the cousins considered the meaning behind his words. After a few moments of uncomfortable silence, Pop spoke again. "I need Tanya to make anotha move."

Ricco blew out a long breath. "C'mon, Pop. Last time she did somethin' for y'all, she got snatched up by them people. No offense, but fuckin' wit' y'all is dangerous."

Pop chuckled. "You got that. But I think this gon' benefit all of us. I heard about J-West and Goon Squad. I dealt wit' niggas like them before, and if we sit back and let them niggas plot and make they moves, it's gon' be too late for us to pop back if they find out who we is. I need Tanya to go wit' Star and Princess to see what these niggas know and how we can hit these niggas if they try some shit."

"Whoa! Whoa! Whoa! Hold on, mane. Goon Squad deadly like AIDS, my nigga. I ain't wit' this and don't want no-parts. We good. And who the fuck is Star? I know you ain't talkin' 'bout that thotty-ass stripper bitch."

"She got involved. They together now. Tanya wanted to call you and let you know, but I told her I would talk to you. Everything already in motion. I thought you'd agree if you heard it from me. Tanya see the big picture. If Goon Squad find out who we is, they comin'."

Ricco grabbed his phone. "Hell nah! Nah! I'm callin' her ass right now. We ain't gettin' in this."

"He right, cuz," Red Dot spoke up. "If Goon Squad find out who y'all is, they gon' sweat shit. It ain't gon' be hard to connect the dots since y'all was together. They plotted on y'all. Y'all gotta use them bitches to find out what them niggas know."

Pop nodded to Red Dot before turning back to Ricco. "Er'body see what's goin' on but you. Whatever you hidin' from, you can't keep hidin'. All that layin' low is over."

"I ain't hidin' from shit. I don't want this shit. I been through all this before. Ain't nothin' good in them streets. I got shot in the face because of it. I ain't trynna lose nothin' else," Ricco vented, tears threatening to spill from his eyes.

"Fuck wit' me, my nigga, and I got you. Tell me who shot you and we can go fuck them niggas up. But right now I need you wit' me and focused on Goon Squad."

Ricco ignored Pop, continuing to try to call his woman. When she didn't answer, he started texting.

"I'll fuck witchu, brah," Red Dot spoke up. "Tell me what I

need to do. I'm ready to get a bag."

Pop studied the small-time hustler. "What happened to Ricco?"

Red Dot turned to his cousin for approval.

"Stay out my bidness, Red Dot!" Ricco growled.

***

"I don't know about this, y'all. I never stripped before," Tanya said, checking her reflection in the full-length mirror. She wore light make-up, hair bone-straight and flowing past her shoulders, her body barely covered by a white one-piece bathing suit.

"All you gotta do is shake ya ass a li'l bit and let me and Princess do all the work," Star said easily, making it seem as if stripping for the first time was no big deal. She was more concerned with adjusting her double-D breasts inside a way-too-small bra.

"That don't make it easy for me. I never danced before. What if they touch me?"

"If you don't like it, tell 'em to stop," Princess spoke up, wrestling her dreadlocks into a ponytail and checking out the way her ass looked in the gold fishnet stockings. "And if you nervous, take one of these percs. They will have yo' ass all the way laid back."

"Ooh! Gimme one," Star said, snatching a pill and swallowing it dry. "I don't' know why Tanya never told me 'bout you. We coulda been out here fuckin' the city up."

A knock on the bathroom door interrupted the women getting ready. "Aye! C'mon out here and shake dat ass! Niggas been waitin' all night!"

"Get away from the door, horny-ass nigga!" Star screamed before turning to Tanya. "Let's get out here and get this money and info. Don't smoke nothin' you don't see get rolled, and don't drink nothin' you don't see get poured."

"And don't do nothin' you don't feel comfortable doin'," Princess added.

When the scantily-clad women revealed themselves, all eyes popped and focused on them. Oohs and ahs filled the room as two men approached Star and Tanya, trying to feel them up. "Move, nigga!" Star snapped, pushing one of the men.

He stumbled backward, barely catching himself from falling. After he caught his balance, a mug flashed on his face and he balled up his fists. "Punk-ass bitch!"

Star threw up her hands in a boxer's stance. "C'mon, nigga! Try me!"

"Chill, Radical!"

The angry man paused at the sound of his name being called, spinning to face the man who called his name. "C'mon, D. You seen that bitch put her hands on me."

Even though he was sitting down, Derion was an imposing man. Standing six feet, two inches with a husky build, bald head, and tattoos all over his face, the big man looked savage. "You put yo' hands on her first. Relax. Smoke somethin'. They came to show us a good time."

After one last glaring look, Radical sat down and sulked.

Princess took a moment to address the crowd to avoid any more misunderstandings. "Don't be trynna feel on us without us sayin' y'all can or try to stick y'all fingers in our ass or pussy. We ain't playin' that shit. Y'all empty them pockets and we gon' put on a show. If y'all act cheap, then y'all gon' get what y'all pay for."

When the girls began dancing, the money began falling. Just like they planned, Princess and Star did most of the work while Tanya collected the money and did a few lap dances. After putting on the erotic show, the women lounged around and kicked it with their company. Star was hugged up with Derion, laughing and smoking. Princess picked Radical to be her victim and sat on his lap, stroking his ego, and Tanya sat between two men who pawed at her body, touching her in all the wrong places. The normally modest woman liked their aggressive hands and vulgar whispers. Under any other circumstances she wouldn't have allowed herself to behave in such a manner, but the Percocet had released her inhibitions. Star and Princess recognized the situation for what it was and kept an eye on their girl.

"Why I ain't neva seen you wit' Star before? Where you been

hidin', girl?" Ricco asked, gripping Princess' thigh.

"I ain't been hidin'. You just ain't been lookin' hard enough."

"Turn out the lights! I'm lookin' for you!" he sang. "But on some real shit, I wanna fuck witchu, luv. Why don't you leave yo' girls and come fuck wit' Goon Squad's finest tonight?"

"I don't think my man would like that."

Radical laughed. "Fuck dat nigga, shawty. I just help pay yo' bills. You sittin' on my dick right now. Cancel dat nigga and fuck witcho boy."

Princess gave the impression she was struggling to make a decision. "I don't know. Y'all niggas hot. I don't wanna get fucked up in some shit that don't got nothin' to do wit' me. If the niggas y'all beefin' wit' seen me, they gon' get on my ass. You cool an' all, but I ain't dyin' over no dick."

"Chill, baby. We got the city on lock. Niggas don't move on us. They shook. We make moves. We the big dogs. Niggas know not to fuck in ours or they get burned."

"Well, what happened at Pole?"

Radical gave a suspicious look. "Whatchu talkin' 'bout?"

Princess gave Radical a look of her own. "The streets talk, and you know dancers hear everything. I heard y'all had a issue."

He laughed. "You always speak yo' mind like this?"

"When it comes to my life, hell yeah! My momma ain't raise no fool."

Radical gave her a long look. "Listen, that shit wasn't 'bout nothin'. My niggas fucked up and got clapped up. When Laro get out the hospital, we gon' find who dem niggas is and take care of that. We Goon Squad, baby.

***

When the key was inserted into the lock, Ricco's good eye found the door. Before it opened, he had crossed the living room and was in Star's face.

"Damn, nigga! Move."

Ricco ignored her and got in Tanya's face. "Fuck yo' ass been?

53

Fuck you ain't text me back?"

"I'm sorry, babe," Tanya slurred, swaying a little. "We had to–"

"Yo' ass high!" he accused. "Fuck you been out there doin'? Where the rest of yo' clothes?"

"Chill, Ricco. Let us in the house first," Princess said.

"Nah! Fuck that! Y'all ain't comin' in here. This my shit. Matter fact, all y'all muthafuckas get out!"

"Chill, brah," Red Dot spoke up. "You wilin' out."

Ricco spun toward his cousin, rage burning inside his good eye. "You can't hear, nigga? Fuck out my shit. You too, Pop Somethin'!"

The tall, muscular goon stood silently and crossed the living room. Ricco felt a bit intimidated by Pop's size, but he didn't let it show. He couldn't show weakness in front of his girl, so he met Pop's stare as they stood face-to-chest.

"Get out cho feelin's, li'l brah. She put in work and they got the job done. You need to congratulate her for her boldness instead of harassin' her for not bein' what you want her to be. She trynna save yo' life, nigga."

After saying his piece, Pop left with everyone else. Ricco slammed the door behind them, then spun to find Tanya. She was lying on the couch. He stormed over and got in her face. "So, this what you on? You don't talk to me about shit? You just do what you wanna do?"

"It wasn't like that, baby. I did this for us."

"How you doin' this for us? We ain't in no drama. That's they shit."

"We is in it. Why didn't you tell me you ran over Laro? Why do you hide everything from me? Why won't you tell me nothin' about you?"

"We ain't finna go there. You know I don't talk about what I been through. And this ain't 'bout me. This 'bout you. Where was you at, and why you dressed like a ho?"

Tanya didn't like being referred to as a ho, so she rolled her eyes and looked away. Ricco took it as her disrespecting him, got mad, and grabbed her by the face. "You hear me talkin' to yo' ass, bitch?"

Tanya snatched away from him. "Let me go, nigga! Don't be puttin' yo' hands on me!"

Ricco got madder. "That's how you talk to yo' man? You big and bad now? You fuck wit' them hos for one night and lose respect for yo' nigga?"

"Fuck you, nigga! You ain't finna be–"

Slap! Tanya fell to the couch, holding her face. Even though she was high, she knew the situation was serious. Ricco had hit her, something she never expected him to do.

Ricco's eyes bulged in shock as he looked from his girlfriend to the palm of his hand. He had lost control and caused pain to the woman he loved. "I'm sorry, baby," he apologized, reaching out to her.

"Get the fuck away from me!" she snapped, slapping his hand away.

Ricco wore the sorrow on his face and in his eye. "I'm sorry, baby. I didn't mean to hit you."

Tanya stood to face him, tears flowing down her cheeks. "You been lyin' to me and keepin' secrets since we met. I accepted that shit and still loved yo' ass. I had yo' baby, and this how you do me? Put yo' hands on me 'cause I'm trynna save yo' ass? You ran Laro over, and he ain't dead. When he get out the hospital, they comin' for us. I heard Goon Squad say it. I ain't finna sit back and let them take my family. But you is. What kinda man is you?"

Ricco couldn't handle the question or the look in her eyes. Like she had lost respect for him. The unbreakable bond had been severed.

"I danced for Goon Squad. I took some pills and got drunk. I shook my ass and gave them niggas lap dances. They gave me three thousand dollars. I did all that for us. 'Cause I love you and don't want nothin' to happen to you. I didn't fuck them niggas. I'm loyal to you. You can trust me, but it's obvious you don't because you still keepin' secrets. I'ma do what I gotta do to take care of our family and get us out these projects. If you love us like you say you do, prove it."

Chapter 6

"I can't stop thinkin' about Queenie," Princess said.

"I know. I think about her, too. I miss my bitch," Pop responded, tenderness in his voice.

"Somebody took her, and it don't make sense. Why would they do that? For money? A ransom?"

"I been thinkin' the same shit. We fucked up so many niggas that it's hard to say who it coulda been."

"It gotta be SOD or Grind Squad. Everybody else dead or we left 'em in Texas."

"SOD ain't got no beef wit' us. They moved on and didn't look back. And Grind Squad just wanted us out the city. I talked to D.D."

"But we killed his brother. If they was plugged as they said, then it could be them. Can't anybody take her from a room being guarded. It was somebody wit' connections."

Pop nodded in agreement. "The more you talk, the more I agree. But we can't go back to Atlanta and just start fuckin' niggas up. The ATL is too hot for us. And too dangerous."

Princess let out a long breath, tears threatening to spill from her eyes. "I know you right, but it just feels like I should be out there trying to find her. What if they torturing her? What if she need us to find her?"

Pop sat up in bed, pulling Princess close. "We gon' get her back, baby. That's my word. But we can't do it right now. First we gotta get stronger. Get stable. Get a team. Then we gon' move. But for now, hold onto yo' emotions. And if the pain too much for you, give it to me and let me carry that burden. Cry if you need to. I got you."

Princess lay her head against Pop's chest and let the tears flow. She cried for the uncertainty of Queenie's whereabouts. She cried for the pain her sister might've endured. And she cried because she might not see her again.

Seeing Princess in such a vulnerable state was having an effect on Pop Somethin'. Her pain was causing him pain. He wanted to protect her, shield her from hurt, harm, and danger. At that moment he would have given anything to see her smile again. And as he kissed the top of her head, he realized he had fallen for Princess. He didn't know when or how, but the love he swore not to get involved in had crept in anyway.

"Damn," Princess cursed when her phone began vibrating.

"Who is it?" Pop asked.

"Radical," she answered after checking the screen.

Pop thought about J-West and Laro. "Answer it. See what he want."

After taking a moment to compose herself and wipe away the tears, Princess answered. "You callin' early."

"It's ten o'clock. Early bird get the first worm. When you trynna get a bag, you get to it. Niggas wit' time ain't got no money. Niggas wit' money ain't got no time."

Princess laughed. "That was slick. So, what up wit' you? You callin' to gimme some money for my time?"

"Hold on, shawty. I ain't no trick. If I bless you, it ain't to pay for yo' time. I'm just lookin' out. I do shit for my people 'cause I love showin' love. I wanna fuck witchu. I told you that. What up?"

Princess looked at Pop and rolled her eyes. "I'm wit' my man right now, and he the jealous type."

"Fuck yo' nigga and his feelin's. I tell you what. Getcho girls and come kick it wit' us later. We gon' bless y'all. That way yo' nigga won't get mad if he know you gettin' that paper. I'ma call you later. Be ready for me."

After ending the call, Princess turned to Pop. "He wanna see us tonight."

"Take care of that. See where he lay his head at and if he talked to Laro. I gotta make a few moves wit' Red Dot."

"You fuckin' wit' him? Is he wit' us?"

"Yeah. Ricco still on his shit, so I'ma take Red Dot as far as I can. He know a few niggas we can put on. I'ma look into it. But I ain't forgot about Ricco. That nigga is the key."

***

"Tell me about these niggas? How good you know 'em?"

"These my niggas. My day-ones," Red Dot said from the passenger seat of the rented Chrysler 300. "Been knowin' 'em since *Blue's Clues*. Dank is a li'l nigga, but he 'bout that action. Goon, you gon' like him. Quan is one of them light-skinned, pretty-boy niggas, but he loyal. And the nigga can flip a eight ball to a ounce in a hour. Paco my Mexican nigga that think he black. He just got out the bing, so he trynna do the right thing. Fuckin' wit' tattoos an' shit. But his cousin, Ghost, got the plug."

Pop Somethin' nodded. "And you sayin' these niggas valid?"

"One hunnit grand."

Pop glanced at the young hustler, his stare serious. "You willin' to put yo' life on the line for these niggas? 'Cause if any fuckery go down, it's on you."

Red Dot took a moment to think over his words. "Yeah. Uh. These my niggas."

"What up wit' the stutter? Anything you need to tell me? I don't like surprises."

"Nah. My niggas is valid, as far as I know. But I know you one of them serious-ass niggas, and I ain't trynna die for no nigga."

Pop had a laugh. "You good, Dot. As long as they good. These yo' niggas, so you responsible for 'em. That's how I move. I need to know if you can handle this. You in or out?"

Red Dot took his time answering. "Yeah. I'm in. I'm ready to eat."

"Good. We gon' get to it. Now, tell me about Ricco. What that nigga runnin' from?"

"He don't want nobody to know about him. He don't want me tellin' his bidness."

"I hear you, and I respect yo' loyalty. But I need to know if what this nigga runnin' from can come bite me in the ass. Tanya and my bitch runnin' 'round makin' moves. I need to know if his issues can come back on me and mine."

Red Dot let out a heavy breath. "Look, brah. All I'ma say is he used to be the plug in Miami. I seen the nigga ridin' 'round wit'

$100,000 cash money. All twenties. I thought that shit was a million dollars. He was up, brah. Then some grimy-ass niggas fucked him over. I don't think he runnin' from the niggas. I think he runnin' from the game."

Ten minutes later, Pop parked the Chrysler and checked his surroundings. One-story brick row houses lined both sides of the street. The screens on the windows looked like black metal grates, and the screen doors were made of heavy, black-painted stainless steel. The buildings looked designed to keep the occupants on the inside locked in and the people on the outside locked out.

"These the Merrywheather Projects, but we call it The Zone. Like the *Twilight Zone*. The shit that go on in these projects is damn near unbelievable. Don't nobody give a fuck about us in here. Not the politicians, the police, or the churches. Shit, the only time twelve come to The Zone is to pick up dead bodies. We goin' to the second building. Dank live here wit' his baby mama."

After a couple raps on the screen door, a deep voice called from inside, "What dat?"

"Red Dot. Open the door, nigga."

Three locks clicked and the door swung open. Dank was a small man, a shade under five-foot-seven with a medium build, but his aura was powerful. When Pop looked in his eyes, he could instantly tell he was in the presence of a real nigga. He had dark skin, a short, nappy afro, a wide nose, big lips, and tattoos covering his neck, chest, and arms. "'Sup witchu, niggas?" he nodded.

Pop nodded in return as he and Red Dot walked into the apartment. Before closing the door, Dank stuck his head outside to make sure everything was how it was supposed to be. When he was satisfied, he closed and locked the door.

Inside the apartment, Paco and Quan were playing *Call of Duty*. Pop sized up everyone. He liked what he'd seen in Dank. The little nigga was a goon. Paco was average height, his brown skin covered with ink. Long French braids hung down his back, and a silver Rosary hung from his neck. Quan looked the part of a pretty boy, light-skinned, hair cut low with brushed waves, snug-fitting designer clothes, gold-rimmed glasses, and three gold chains around his neck.

"Aye, pause that weak-ass game. This who I was tellin' y'all 'bout," Red Dot said, getting everyone's attention. "We gotta holla."

Quan sat the controller down reluctantly, eyeing Pop. "This betta be important, brah. If it ain't, Red Dot, I'm whoopin' yo' ass. And you a big nigga, but my knuckle game nice," he joked.

Pop Somethin' mugged him hard, staring Quan in the eyes until he looked away. "I don't play no games. Especially wit' niggas I don't know. If you wanna play, leave. Niggas get killed for playin' too much."

The house grew quiet as everyone digested his words, unsure how to respond. Pop's size and tone had intimidated everyone. Except Dank. He began laughing.

"That's what yo' square-ass get, nigga! 'Bout time we got anotha real nigga on deck."

"Y'all see brah don't play no games," Red Dot spoke up. "Chill wit' the jokes. This shit serious. I told him y'all was valid, and he wanna fuck wit' us. Y'all in?"

"No disrespect, but who is he? How you know him?" Dank asked.

Red Dot was about to answer, but Pop waved him off. "I'm from Texas. Shit got live and I set that bitch on fire before I left. I landed here and made a few connections. I heard a nigga can check a bag here, and I wanna run it up. I don't know the city like y'all, so I need a team. Red Dot movin' wit' me, and he said y'all his niggas. I'm offerin' y'all spots. But just know I get down for mine, and I play for keeps."

"How much paper we talkin' 'bout?" Paco asked. "If we ain't playin' wit' birdies, I'm out. I ain't riskin' my freedom for a couple racks. I'd rather do tattoos and get pussy."

"I wanna start small to see what y'all capable of. All y'all get a half bird. If shit go right, we jumpin' in the big leagues."

Hearing they would all be getting eighteen ounces of dope got Quan's attention. "When do we get the work? How much you want back?"

"We ain't gon' worry 'bout that right now. First things first. Paco, can you get two birdies from yo' cousin? I heard you can get a plug. And is this enough for you to join the team?"

The French braid-wearing Latino smiled up at Pop Somethin'. "Hell yeah. Both ways. I'm in, and I can get us a plug."

"Take care of that. Get at me when you get the numbers. Now we gotta talk shop," Pop said, pausing to look at Dank. "We gotta getcho family outta The Zone. We finna take over, and this gon' be ground zero."

Dank nodded, a wide smile growing on his face and murder in his eyes. "Hell yeah! I neva like these niggas 'round here anyway. Let's bad these bitch-ass niggas."

"Hold on. Wait," Quan cut in. "I got a line, and my shit slappin' like a pay phone. I don't gotta bag nobody."

"It don't work like that," Red Dot spoke up. "This where we settin' up at. Fuck yo' plans. We a team now. We eat together. If you want the product, you gotta put in the work. Or leave."

"Damn, brah. It's other ways to eat. We can't go to war and get money."

"Who said anything about a war?" Pop cut in. "We gon' slaughter these niggas State Property-style. Get down or lay down. Then we movin' in. If niggas ain't sellin' our shit, they ain't sellin' shit. Either you in or out. It's that simple."

All eyes flocked to Quan. He visibly cringed under their stares. "I'm in. You niggas ain't finna eat without me. Plus, don't none of you niggas know how to whip that work like me."

Pop looked to Red Dot to see what he thought. The gold-toothed hustler nodded in approval. Then Pop addressed his new team. "I hear it's pretty much open season out here. Niggas hustle how they want. Ain't nobody claimed this project yet. We gon' do that. Red Dot told me 'bout Link and his niggas. Since they the most known and recognized, we gon' hit them first. Then Prada and his niggas. We ain't givin' 'em no options. We pushin' they shit back and kickin' 'em out. The rest of these petty hustlin' over. Goon-style."

Chapter 7

"You know my sister gon' fuck you up if she find out we doin' this," Katrina said as she lay across the bed. "I don't think you should record it."

Link sat on the dresser holding his phone and puffing the blunt, anxiously waiting for the nineteen-year-old to begin the show. The young Puerto Rican bombshell had the hustler's nose open. Reddish brown skin, big breasts, thick thighs, and a phat ass made Link betray his baby momma's trust and start fucking her sister on the side.

"Kandy got betta shit to worry 'bout than who I'm fuckin'. And she know not to touch my phone," Link said, tapping the blunt's ashes on the floor. "I gotta have both of y'all. You do shit for me that she can't. And I do shit for you that no do shit otha nigga can. Yo' Camaro got new rims. I'ma get that apartment soon as I make my next flip. Now quit talkin' and let me see yo' fuck faces."

Katrina opened her legs wide, exposing her bald, pink pussy. "I swear to god, you bet not show nobody."

"Quit playin', girl. You know I ain't finna show nobody this video. This for me when you not around. Show me that pussy mine. Cum for me."

Katrina lifted her head, grabbing her breasts and sucking the nipples. With her other hand she fingered her clitoris, giving Link a seductive stare. The erotic scene had him so turned on that he reached for his tool and began jacking off. The secret lovers continued the self-pleasure until loud noises got their attention.

Pop, pop, pop, pop, pop, pop!
Boom, boom, boom, boom, boom!

"Is they shootin'?" Katrina panicked, going for her clothes.

"Stay here! Don't move!" Link said, grabbing his clothes and the .357 revolver.

***

Man-Man, Killa, and Seven stood in front of the row of houses in The Zone, passing a blunt around. The men were regulars in the projects and at one point had called the place home. Today they no longer lived in the projects, but it was still their hood. It was where they hustled, played, and preyed. And tonight it was no different. Except they didn't know they had become prey.

"I should send Kandy a video of they ass. Then she gon' be done fuckin' with dat nigga and I can slide in that juice box," Man-Man laughed.

Killa shook his head. "That's some sucka-ass shit, hatin'-ass nigga. Go find yo' own bitch."

"Have you niggas took a look at Kandy?" Man-Man asked rhetorically "She super bad! A twenty piece. I wanna add her to my list. And if I gotta hate, so what? At least I'ma fuck. Link got a bad bitch, and he fuckin' her over."

"Shut that weak-ass shit up!" Seven frowned. "How the fuck you knew that nigga this long and hatin'?"

"Power of the P-U-S-S-Y," Killa said. "That shit be havin' these weak-minded-ass niggas ready to fold. Type-a nigga thata snitch to get out of jail so he can get back to the pussy faster."

Man-Man got mad. "Now you niggas goin' too far! I ain't no snitch, soft-ass nigga. I ain't neva told on nobody. Fuck you talkin' 'bout?"

"Whatchu think you doin' by sendin' Kandy the video of Link and Katrina? You a snitch, nigga," Killa said.

"You betta watchcho—"

Boom!

Killa and Seven watched in confusion and horror as a chunk of Man-Man's head exploded, splashing them with brains, blood, and gray matter. When they realized he had been shot, it was too late for them to run or shoot back. All they could do is watch in frozen terror as four men charged them, firing semi automatic weapons. The bodies of The Zone's regulars jerked and spasmed as they were filled with hot metal.

Inside the apartment, three men lounged around smoking weed, drinking and playing video games. When the shooting began, all of them froze, wondering if their niggas outside were doing the shooting or under attack. When the front door opened, they got their answer. A big man walked into the apartment holding a large pistol in each hand. Behind him was a shorter man with an assault rifle. Two more armed men follow in the rear. None of the intruders hesitated as they squeezed triggers on their weapons.

When the three occupants of the house lay on the floor bleeding, the big man addressed his team. "We gotta check the rest of the house." Pop whispered. "Red Dot and Paco, y'all check the back. Dank, come wit' me."

After they split up, Pop and Dank went to check the bedrooms. The first one was empty. When they came to the second door, both men paused, sensing someone behind the door. After making eye contact, they each gave a nod. No words were needed. Pop Somethin' kepi his back to the wall, remaining hidden as he pushed the door open.

Boom, boom, boom, boom, boom, boom, boom!
Click! Click!

When they heard the firing pin clicking against empty shell casing, Pop Somethin' and Dank moved at the same time. The compact street soldier stepped into the room first, his SK firing, sending bullets into Link's face and chest. Katrina stood next to the bed, a sheet wrapped around her naked body, screaming in terror. Pop Somethin's 50 caliber barked once. The Desert Eagle bullet smacked her between the eyes, silencing the scream.

***

"Y'all heard what happened to Link an' 'em?" Dru asked, his eyes wide with shock and fear.

Prada wore a smug look as he stepped from the G-Wagon Benz. Standing a little over six feet and 260 pounds, the big man looked indestructible and unshakable. "Nah. Don't tell me the feds got on that nigga ass."

"Nah, brah. That nigga dead."

The giant of a man stopped in his tracks, stunned. "Link dead?"

Dru nodded his head up and down, a hint of worry in his eyes.

"Yeah. Him and his niggas. Bodies all around they spot. Look like some shit out a scary movie."

The look on Prada's face changed from stunned to worried. "When this happen? How you know?"

"I just came from over there. I heard the shootin'. Shit sounded like a war poppin' off."

"And you sure Link got knocked off?"

"Not for sure, nah. I didn't go in the house. But I seen Killa and Seven on the ground for sure, and you know all them niggas day-ones."

"Damn," Prada muttered in disbelief. "Fuck them niggas do that got they shit sweated like that?"

"I don't know, but I think we need to get the fuck outta here. Twelve finna tape this bitch off and prolly do a sweep."

"Yeah. I just gotta run in the trap and get my other phone. Where Tycoon and Drill at?"

"They in the house. I already told them what happened. We was waitin' on you to come back."

"A'ight. We gon' get the fuck outta here and fall back for a couple days. See what the streets sayin'. See who the fuck brought heat to them niggas and why."

Prada looking in all directions, staying on point as they walked to their trap. As he stood on the porch, he couldn't shake the feeling he was being watched. His hand stayed near his waist as Dru unlocked the door. When it opened, he took one last look before going inside.

A hundred yards away, at the edge of the row houses, Pop Somethin' and his clique of killers blended in with the night. Watching. Waiting. Lurking.

"You see how that nigga was on point'? He a hawk. Big-ass nigga don't miss shit," Dank pointed out.

Pop leaned against the wall, agreeing with Dank's observation. "I seen all that. You a sharp li'l nigga."

"I'm nineteen, but I know the streets like I ran through 'em in a past life."

"Good. 'Cause this one gon' be harder than the last one. It look like the li'l nigga put Prada on point. We ain't gon' be able to hit they spot 'cause we lost the element of surprise. We gon' have to wait 'em out. Dank, take Paco 'round the back and y'all wait on the other side of the building. I'ma keep Red Dot wit' me and—"

"Here they come!" Dank whispered.

Pop looked toward the trap as six men walked out, Dru and Prada following in the rear. All of them wore serious faces and looked around anxiously as they walked quickly down the walkway. Pop knew the hit would be hard. They were outnumbered six to four. The only thing in their favor was they already had their guns drawn. It was now or never.

"Let's go," Pop whispered, charging around the building with both Desert Eagles firing. The 50-caliber slugs blazed toward their targets faster than the speed of sound, slamming into the lead man's chest. He stumbled backward, fear and shock spreading across his mug before he fell to the ground.

Immediately after Pop rounded the building, his goons followed, all of their guns firing, sending heated death toward Prada and his niggas.

When Prada seen the big, black-clothed figure round the corner of the building, he knew death was close. And as far as he was concerned, he was too young to die. Death would have to wait. He reacted quickly, pulling the FYN from his waist. The fully automatic hand pistol had a thirty-round clip, and Prada had another one in his pocket. The streets had trained him for moments like these.

The FYN erupted, sending bullets at three rounds a second toward his enemies. The Zone sounded like a battlefield when his niggas got their hearers out and began shooting back. Hot lead flew indiscriminately as three of Prada's niggas went down. The other three held their own, forcing Pop and his niggas to take cover against the buildings.

Pop took a knee to reload his Desert Eagles. When he looked up again, he spotted Prada backing away, firing wildly. Pop knew he couldn't let him get away. To kill a snake, he had to chop off the head.

"Take are of these niggas," Pop called to Dank. "I'm goin' after Prada."

Dank nodded right before he stood and continued shooting the chopper. Pop Somethin' moved carefully from his position as bullets whizzed all around. He spotted Prada ducked down, reloading his pistol.

Pop took aim just as Prada looked up. He knew he wouldn't be able to get out of the way before the Desert Eagle bullets got to him, so he did the only thing he could, grabbing his worker who was ducking next to him.

Pop let loose with the hand cannon, hitting up the man Prada used for a shield. And instead of folding, Prada upped the FYN and began firing back. Pop watched the sparks fly in his direction as four bullets slammed into his chest, knocking him to the ground and taking his breath away. When he looked up again, Prada was on the move, disappearing behind a building.

Red Dot, Dank, and Paco had surrounded the soul survivor and gunned him down when Red Dot seen Pop get hit up. "Awe, shit!" he cursed, running toward his fallen leader. "Pop! You good?"

The big man grunted as he struggled to stand. "That bitch-nigga good," Pop breathed, rubbing at the stinging slugs lodged in his bullet-proof vest. "We made our point. Let's get the fuck outta here."

***

"Damn, gurl! What happened to yo' face?" Princess frowned.

"I know Ricco ain't put his hands on you?" Star asked.

Tanya reached for her face as she sat in the passenger seat of Star's BMW. "Me and Ricco got into it after y'all left."

"I'ma shoot that nigga other eye out!" Princess said, going for the door handle and the gun in her purse.

"I'ma cut the nigga dick off!" Star added, also reaching for her purse.

"No!" Tanya screamed. "I don't need y'all to fight my battles. I got it. He jealous and insecure right now. He used to me bein' a submissive house wife. Before y'all came, everything he said was the way it went. I didn't know nothin' and hadn't seen shit. But being around y'all and seein' and doin' things I never did is openin' the world up to me. He don't like' it, but I need this. I gotta find out who I am. I can't do that if I always let him tell me what to do. I made up my mind last night that I'ma live my life the way I want. I'm not gon' do nothin' to intentionally hurt my man, but I gotta do what I gotta do. And right now I gotta keep my family safe and get us out these raggedy-ass apartments."

Princes let go of the gun, eyeing her cousin proudly. "Damn, bitch. You was listenin' to Michele Obama speeches last night?"

"Fuck that shit. You can't be lettin' that nigga put his hands on you," Star spat. "I think we should go jump his ass."

"Would you stop, Star? Damn!" Tanya snapped. "I said I got it. Plus, Ricco at work, and y'all ain't finna do nothin' to my man."

"If you woulda shown that same toughness last night, Ricco might not-a punched yo' ass," Star sassed, rolling her eyes.

The reunited friends had a stare down.

"Would y'all stop?" Princess intervened. "She said she got it, Star. Let her handle her business. She a big girl now."

Star rolled her eyes and put the car in drive. "Whatever."

"Quit actin' stank!" Princess laughed.

Star shook her head and breathed deep as she steered her car. "You Texas bitches is gettin' on my nerves."

"Fuck you wit' a big-ass dildo, you Jacksonville ho," Tanya teased. "Now, can we go get these niggas' money? Ricco workin' overtime and Yanna wit' a babysitter. I need to make enough to pay first and last months' rent and buy some new furniture. I want my family in a new house by next week."

The women ended up in a luxury hotel suite. Only three Goon Squad members were present: Radical, Derion, and Flex. A portable pole had been set up in the entertainment room, and Star was upside down on it, doing tricks. Princess sat on Radical's lap, giving him a lap dance and watching her friend. Tanya sat on Flex's lap, doing the same.

"A'ight. I seen enough ass-shakin'," Derion said. "I wanna see some live shit. I got twenty-five hunnit. G'on, do somethin' to impress me. What else y'all got in that trick bag?"

The women exchanged glances before Princess got up and grabbed the bag Derion spoke of. After taking out a fourteen-inch double-sided dildo, she walked over to Star. "You know what to do wit' this?"

Star looked from the big, black snake to Derion. "It's gon' take more than twenty-five hunnit to see what I can do wit' that. Quit bein' cheap. Pay to play."

"Radical and Flex gon' make up the difference, and we gon' give y'all five racks. It betta be a good show."

After satisfied looks, Princess and Star stood face-to-face and took an end of the dildo into their mouths. The men watched in lustful excitement as the sexperts took more and more of the sex toy into their mouths. Their lips touched in a slippery kiss when they deep-throated both sides.

When they felt the men had seen enough, Star lay on the floor on her back, opening her legs. Princess moved in and began sucking Star's clit while fucking her with the big, black snake. Star moaned in pleasure, palming the back of Princess' head, loving the sight of a woman eating her pussy. And not only did she love the sight of a woman eating her, but she also loved the tonguing she was getting.

Princess knew what she was doing and brought her to a quick orgasm. When Star gathered herself, Princess spun around on all fours and Star began licking her ass while fucking her from behind with the dildo. Princess lifted her head toward the ceiling, closing her eyes and moaning in pleasure. The tongue in her ass and dildo in her pussy had her in a zone of pleasure.

When Star's hand became covered in cum, she called Tanya over for help holding the dildo while she got on her hands and knees behind Princess. After a little hesitation, Tanya slipped an end of the dildo into Princess and Star's pussies and held it in place as they threw their asses back. The women performed like porn stars, moaning in pleasure, smashing Tanya's hand between their phat asses as they fucked the dildo. The newcomer was so turned on by the show that she began fingering herself.

The sex show lasted an hour, Star a Princess getting off several times and giving the men a show worth their money. "That shit was nasty and sexy as fuck!" Star said, looking at Princess like she wanted to fuck some more as they freshened up in the bathroom.

"We had them niggas gone!" Princess smiled. "One day we gon' finish it wit' the real thing. My nigga would love to fuck yo' ass."

"Just say when. I betcha that big, black-ass nigga got a big dick," Star laughed. "And did you see Tanya playin' wit' that pussy while we was fuckin'? Bitch gettin' turned out!"

"Y'all had my ass horny and ready to fuck," Tanya blushed. "I was watchin' them niggas watch y'all. They was mesmerized. Niggas didn't even wanna blink. Y'all had 'em under a spell. I ain't neva seen no shit like that. I wish I could have niggas hypnotized like that."

"You can," Star said. "It's a gold mine between yo' legs."

"Niggas will do anything for pussy. That's why you can't be just givin' it away. What's between yo' legs is worth more than all the money in the world. You fuck a nigga the right way and you can get anything you want," Princess added.

"That's why I love bein' a stripper. I can shake my ass or suck or fuck a nigga and have him actin' like my bitch. These bum bitches hate on strippers 'cause they scared to do what we do. They call us hos 'cause they scared and insecure about they bodies and looks. But sex is power. Being sexy is powerful. You see how we had them niggas. Now we finna go get they ass to tell us everything we wanna know."

Tanya looked at Princess and Star in awe. "I want to know how to do what y'all do. I wanna know how to make niggas do what I want 'em to do."

"And you will. Stick wit' us. We got you," Princess said.

A knock on the door interrupted their girl chat. "What?" Star answered, irritation in her voice.

"Open the door," Derion called.

When Tanya opened the door, he barged in, staring at Star with lust in his eyes. "Me and Star need to holla. They want y'all out there."

Star nodded to her girls, letting them know it was okay to leave.

When Tanya and Princess walked in the entertainment room, Radical and Flex perked up like they had just snorted lines of coke. "Damn, 'bout time y'all back," Flex said.

"You actin' like you didn't enjoy the show," Tanya smiled.

"I did. Now I want that one-on-one show," he grinned, pulling he onto his lap.

While Tanya and Flex flirted and got touchy-feely, Princess sat next to Radical, remaining subdued.

"What up, baby? Let's go to the room and put on our own show," Radical smiled lustfully, grabbing her thigh.

Princess let him touch, but refused to move from the couch. "I told you I got a nigga. You cool, but I ain't trynna go there witchu. Plus, y'all niggas is too hot."

Radical let out a frustrated breath. "C'mon, shawty. Why we gotta do this er'time we kick it? You just fucked yo' girl in front of me and my niggas, and now you trippin'? Where dey do dat at?"

"That as entertainment. I'm 'bout a check. Fuckin' you is different. I got a nigga. And I don't feel safe witchu. Y'all in plenty shit."

"First of all, fuck your nigga. You here wit' me. And what you talkin' this safe shit for? You good. I told you, niggas know what it is."

"But what about what happened at Pole? Two of yo' niggas got killed. What if they lookin' for you? If I get seen wit'–"

"C'mon, shawty. Two of my niggas ain't dead. Only one did. Laro fucked up, but he a'ight. We holla'ed, and we know who did that shit. We gon' catch them niggas and dead that shit."

"I don' know," Princess hesitated. "Who is the niggas? Tell me what they look like so I can watch out, too."

Radical gave her a suspicious look. "You doin' too much, shawty. I got you. You good."

Princess' hand went to Radical's thigh, inching close to his dick. "If you wanna fuck me, I need to feel safe. Only way that's gon' happen is if I know what to look out for. I know how this shit go out in the streets, and I ain't trynna get caught up in that. I ain't dyin' for no dick. If you wanna fuck wit' me, tell me."

Radical gave it some thought, and then he smiled. "You a sexy muthafucka, you know that? If yo' ass wasn't so bad, I'da been putcho ass out. But I want you. The nigga drive a black Lambo. Big, black-ass nigga wit' dreads and a Rick Ross beard. If you see that car, call me."

Princess' heart jumped when he actually told her, but on the outside she remained cool, leaning close and pecking Radical on the lips. "That wasn't so hard, now was it? I feel safer already. And when I feel safe, my pussy get wet."

Radical licked his lips. "Well, let's go have a meetin' in my bedroom then!"

J-Blunt

Chapter 8

The wetness around Ricco's dick stirred him awake. He looked down and seen Tanya's head bobbing up and down, her jaws wrapped tightly around his tool. He wanted to push her head away and snap on her ass for staying out late again. It was the third time this week, and he was pissed. But when she moved her mouth to his balls and began sucking while jacking him off, he decided to hold his ire until he busted a nut. She was giving some bomb-ass head, and he wanted to ride it out.

Then another thought jumped into his mind. Where did she learn to suck dick like this? In a matter of weeks she had gone from an amateur to Super Head. Was she fucking somebody else? Selling pussy? She had to be. That was the only way to explain the new house, furniture, and staying out all night.

The anger began rising. And so did his nut. When Tanya's lips found his tool again, he busted in her mouth. "Awe, shit!" Ricco grunted.

Tanya continued sucking, swallowing his seed. When he went limp, she sucked him hard again.

Ricco was blown away by his girl's head game. Then thoughts of her sucking another man's dick crept into his head. "Wait. Stop," he said, grabbing her head.

Tanya looked up at him, her eyes glossy and red. She was high and horny. "I can't stop," she moaned, crawling up his body.

"Wait. We gotta talk. Where the fuck you–"

Tanya smashed her lips onto his, shoving her tongue in his mouth.

Ricco turned his head, breaking the kiss. "Chill! What the fuck wrong witchu?"

Tanya continued kissing the side of his face and neck. "Can we talk later? I need this right now. I can't wait."

Ricco tried to push her away. "I ain't playin', Tanya. Stop."

She didn't stop. Instead, she grabbed his dick and sat down on it. "We gon' talk later, baby. I promise. I need some dick. I need you. I miss you. I love you."

When her lips found his again, Ricco gave in, kissing her back, not caring that she had just swallowed his nut. He missed her body as much as she missed his. They hadn't fucked in two weeks. His hands gripped her ass and thighs as she rode him. When she was really in the zone, Tanya broke the kiss, lifting her head toward the ceiling, moaning his name. Ricco watched his woman's face. Her eyes were closed, mouth open, saying his name, lost in her own world of pleasure. When her nails began digging into the skin of his chest, he knew she was close to cumming.

And then it came. She dug her nails deeper into his chest, crying out as her orgasm passed through her body. Then she fell on Ricco's chest, panting heavily, breathing deep. Ricco kissed her atop the head and rubbed her back while she gathered herself.

"I don't wanna fight no more," Tanya whispered, keeping her head on his chest.

Ricco heard her, but kept quiet. He didn't know what to say. They had just fucked, and she was vulnerable and open, but he wasn't. He was still mad.

"Did you hear me?" she asked, lifting her head to look at his face.

"Yeah. I heard you," he said flatly.

"I want us to go back to being in love. Being a family. You don't have nothin' to say?"

There was so much he wanted to say. So many questions he wanted to ask. But first he had to know. "Is you fuckin' somebody else?"

"No. I told you I would never cheat on you. I'm in love with you. Only you."

"What up wit' this freaky-ass shit all of a sudden? Where you learn to suck dick like that?"

Tanya looked bashful. "I was so fuckin' horny. And I been gettin' tips from Princess and Star. They told me some shit that I had to try. I'm not cheatin' on you, baby. And I never will."

Ricco studied her with his good eye, trying to find a lie in her tone or face. All he got was an unblinking stare, and the longer he looked, the more he realized the woman lying on top of him wasn't the same one who had his daughter. "You seem different. I feel like I don't know you no more. You stay out I all night. We don't talk. You comin' up wit' money to get us a new crib and furniture. What's goin' on?"

"I told you I was gon' do what I had to do to get us out them raggedy-ass apartments. That's what I been doin'. Since I been kickin' it wit' Star and Princess, I feel like I'm findin' out who I am. What I want. What I'm capable of. Before they came, I was all about you and Yanna. I let you be the man, but inside I wasn't happy. I didn't want to live in the hood and struggle. I wanted to do more than stay home with the baby. But I couldn't talk to you about it because you expected me to be a certain way. And you kept secrets."

"But I liked who you was. I knew you."

"But I didn't like who I was."

"So who is you now? What you do at night? You a stripper? An escort? Now you the one keepin' secrets."

"Just like you," Tanya said. "Now you see how it feels. All this time we been together and I never met yo' family except Red Dot. Is Ricco Turbin even yo' real name? Why won't you tell me what happened to yo' face or talk about yo' past?"

"Because the less you know, the better."

"Well, that's how I feel. I put us in a nice house and I'm not cheatin' on you."

Ricco let out a long breath, thinking on his woman's words. "A'ight. You really wanna do this, we can. I love you, Tanya, and I don't wanna fight no more, either. Ask me anything."

Tanya sat up straighter, studying his face. Her hand went to the wound on the side of his head. "What happened?"

"I got set up," he answered flatly.

Tanya frowned. "I thought we was opening up?"

Ricco took his time responding. "I got set up by a female I was trynna fuck. Her nigga went to jail, and I thought I could slide in. The whole time she was preyin' on me. Her and her niggas took my family hostage. I thought if I gave 'em the money they would let us go. But they didn't. They had already killed my day-one, who it turned out was fuckin' my girl. Then once I gave 'em the money, they killed my girl and my shorty. The bitch shot me in the face, too. They thought I was dead. Shit, I did, too, until I woke up in the hospital. When I healed up, I moved to Jacksonville for a new start. I just wanted to be a simple nigga and live the right way. Then I met you. The reason I didn't talk about my past was 'cause I tried to protect you. The streets is evil. I don't wanna lose nobody else that I love."

Tanya stared at her man like she was seeing him for the first time. She felt sorry for him. He lost his family and found out his girl was cheating with his friend. And he almost died. "Damn, baby. I'm sorry for everything that happened to you. I didn't think it was that bad."

"But that ain't all. My name ain't Ricco. It's Ricardo Ayala. And I ain't black. I'm Dominican. In Miami, I used to be that nigga. They called me Super Trap."

***

"'Bout time you came out the closet, nigga!" Red Dot laughed. "I don't know why you was trynna act like you wasn't no trap star. Nigga, yo' name Super Trap."

"C'mon, nigga. Quit playin'. I'm Ricco. I ain't trynna trap no more. That shit over."

"You mean to tell me that you cool wit' yo' girl goin' out there an' shakin' her ass for niggas? Fifty niggas grab her ass and titties and then she come home to you. How you know she ain't doin' a little extra on the side?"

Ricco mugged his cousin. "Quit playin' wit' me like that."

"C'mon, cuz. Get outcho titty nipples for a minute and hear me out. Tanya bad, brah. Been bad, but didn't nobody know 'cause she was a plain Jane. But now she fuckin' wit' them professional hos and she steppin' her game up. She model status, my nigga. I ain't the only one that noticed."

"Yeah, yeah. My girl bad. I know."

"But that ain't my point. What I'm sayin' is she out there

shakin' her ass 'cause you don't wanna get out there and make it happen. So she usin' what she got to get to it. Don't that make you feel some type of way? She got drive. She want better for the fam. And she makin' it happen."

Ricco sat back in the new leather chair his girl bought with the money she made from shaking her ass. Truth was, it was killing him that Tanya was a stripper. He felt less of a man, no~ being able to provide. His voice had a tremble when he responded, his emotions spilling. "Ever since she told me how she get it, that shit been fuckin' me up, cuz. I feel, like, super lame. As a man, I know I gotta take care of my family. And I thought I was doin' that by bein' a nine-to-five nigga. By bein' there to spend time wit' my girl and daughter. Most street niggas don't understand the importance of time. That shit more important than money."

"But that don't mean you move yo' family to the PJs and get comfortable strugglin'. Yo' bitch want more. Yo' daughter gon' eventually want more. And you can't do shit for them as no janitor."

Ricco let out a little laugh. "I see what you trynna do, nigga. Nah, I ain't fuckin' wit' y'all niggas. Pop Somethin' crazy. The nigga name is Pop Somethin'. He kill niggas everywhere he go. Him and Princess hot as fuck."

"We took over a project, my nigga. A whole fuckin' project! Eight blocks of hundreds of row houses. All ours. Yeah, that nigga crazy. But he also a genius. Didn't they say Albert Einstein was crazy? Bein' crazy is part of bein' a genius. And we need you, brah. We need what you got upstairs. You turned a eight-ball to a Maybach. We got bricks, my nigga. Come help us build a brick house."

Ricco grew silent. Thinking. Wrestling with the decision to remain a janitor or chase a bag. Tanya was his heart. His pride. His joy. His better half. And she was sharing her goods with the world for a couple thousand dollars. He needed to step up, but the risks in the game wasn't worth the rewards. It cost too much. "I can't, brah. Money not worth my life."

After speaking his mind, Ricco got up and went to the kitchen.

Red Dot pulled out his phone and made a call.

"What's good, my nigga?" Pop Somethin' answered.

"I'm in this nigga head," Red Dot smiled. "All he need is a little more push. Is er'thang valid on yo' side?"

"Yeah. We waitin' on y'all."

"Say no more. We on our way."

"Who is we?" Ricco asked, walking in the living room.

"I need a ride, brah. Pop Somethin' on some bullshit and don't wanna come get me."

"C'mon, man. I ain't trynna go out there. Call a cab."

"Damn, nigga. Quit actin' like a sucka. I'll give you some gas money."

"Fuck you. I don't need yo' gas money."

"I forgot. You got that stripper money now. You a baller," Red Dot laughed.

Ricco mugged him. "What I tell you 'bout playin' so much?"

"A'ight, cuz. Just gimme a ride so I can get back to this paper."

Ricco stared at Red Dot seriously for a few moments before smiling. "Damn, you a square-ass nigga. C'mon, man."

Twenty minutes later Ricco parked the Ford Fusion in front of a set of row houses in The Zone. Even though it was late, people hung out on porches and the projects looked to be alive with action.

"You wanna come in and kick it wit' the homies for a second?" Red Dot offered.

"Nah, I'm good. Y'all do y'all thang. I'm goin' home."

"You sure you don't wanna come in?" Red Dot asked, his stare lingering like he knew somethin' Ricco didn't.

"Yeah, nigga. I'm sure. Get the fuck out so I can go home."

"Tanya up in there."

That got Ricco's attention. "Quit playin', nigga, 'fore I whoop yo' ass."

"I ain't playin'. Tanya in there. She workin'."

A darkness spread across Ricco's face, and his top lip began to twitch. "On everything you love, she in there right now?"

"Yeah. She puttin' on a show wit' Princess and Star."

Ricco put the car in park and snatched the key from the

ignition. "Which apartment?"

Red Dot turned to hide the smile on his face as he opened the passenger door. "The first building. Follow me."

When they walked in the apartment, Ricco was smacked in the face by a cloud of weed smoke and loud music. About fifteen niggas stood and lounged around on couches in the living room. They were watching the half-naked women shaking ass and dancing on the floor. Ricco's eyes immediately found his woman. She was giving a lap dance to a fat, dark-skinned nigga who didn't believe in keeping his hands to himself.

When Tanya seen her man, she froze, unable to look at him. Ricco, on the other hand, couldn't take his eyes off her. Seeing the man's hands all over his woman sent a fire through his bones.

"Super Trap! What's good, nigga?" Pop called, walking over to embrace the brokenhearted man.

"What up, Pop?" Ricco mumbled. continuing to stare at Tanya.

Pop Somethin' spun to see what had Ricco's attention. Tanya was still bumping and grindin' on the fat man. "Don't trip on that, li'l brah. She workin'. Gettin' that bag."

"I know," Ricco mugged as jealous rage coursed through him.

"Have a seat. Watch the show. You want somethin' to drink?"

"Nah, I'm good. I'm 'bout to leave. I just wanted to step in to look around."

"Don't leave now, cuz." Red Dot spoke up. "Watch a li'l bit of the show. You gotta see what they do wit' this big-ass black dildo."

Ricco finally took his eyes off his girl, mugging Red Dot. "Who do somethin' wit a dildo?"

Ricco was about to snap on his cousin, but Pop Somethin' pulled him away and they walked away, whispering. His eyes went back to Tanya as she was attempting to get up from the fat man's lap.

"Hold on, baby. Don't leave. You got my dick hard as fuck!" he said, pulling her arm.

Tanya yanked away from him. "Dance over, nigga. Let go."

He grabbed her around the waist and pulled her back onto his lap. "I got fifty more. But this time let me play wit' that pussy."

Tanya tried to stand. "No. Let me go. I'm good,"

The lust-consumed thug pulled her onto his lap again. "Hold on, bitch. You ain't finna take my money and not gimme what I want. I gave you two hunnit already. You ain't done yet."

"Stop! Let me go, nigga!" Tanya said, looking toward Ricco. He stood across the room, watching. A rage building inside him like he never felt.

"Fuck you then, bitch!" the fat man said before slapping her on the ass and giving her a hard shove. Tanya stumbled forward, falling face-first to the floor.

Princess moved to help her cousin while Star confronted the man. "Bitch-ass nigga, don't be puttin' yo' hands on my gurl!"

"Or what?" he asked smugly, showing no concern for the disrespect.

While the commotion was taking place, Ricco walked over to Red Dot and snatched the pistol from the front of his pants. Without hesitation, he walked over to the nigga that disrespected his girl, pointed the gun in his face, and pulled the trigger.

Pow!

Everyone froze, trying to digest what they had just witnessed. Ricco stood over the fallen man, holding the gun, watching the blood drip from his forehead and life drain from his eyes. Then he spoke.

"I'm in. Super Trap back."

Chapter 9

Two Months Later

The late morning sunlight crept through the edges of the closed blinds, illuminating the love nest just enough to see the outline of a pair of naked bodies. Shanice lay in bed, the fuzzy feelin' of a new kind of love exciting all of her senses. She had finally found happiness. Love. Contentment. Satisfaction. All the emotions and feelings she'd experienced with C-Note had been found again. Being in love once was amazing. To experience that same feeling with two people in one year was a miracle. God had answered the brokenhearted prayers, giving her a love that she loved everything about. Especially the way their dark- and light-skinned bodies molded into one like the Chinese Yin and Tang symbol.

Shanice traced fingertips along her lover's body, starting at the clean-shaven bald head, down the shoulders and back, stopping to lightly finger the indentations and scars.

"That feels so good."

Shanice smiled at the sound of her new love's voice. "Hey, baby. Good mornin'."

Queenie opened her eyes, smiling at the woman who had become her rock, nurturer, and healer. "I don't ever get tired of waking up to the sound of yo' voice. Damn, you beautiful."

Shanice blushed, rubbing Queenie's bald head as they shared a morning kiss. "And I don't ever get tired of kissing your soft lips every morning."

"I thought you didn't like girls."

Shanice giggled, leaning in for another kiss. "I don't like 'em. I love you. These two months have been amazing. I can't remember a time when I felt this much contentment and peace. I been fuckin' wit' no-good niggas my whole life trynna find this. Never thought I would find it with a woman. Damn, I love yo' ass."

Queenie didn't respond right away, just stared into Shanice's brown eyes, seeing the love being reflected. "Damn. You wake up beautiful. And all those niggas was just practice for the rear thing.

Sometimes you don't know what's been missin' 'til you get exposed to it."

The light-skinned woman smiled at the compliment, wanting more. When she didn't get it, anger flashed in her eyes as she moved to get out of bed. "That's all you gotta say?"

Queenie sat up, wrapping her arms around Shanice's waist, kissing her on the back. "C'mon, baby. Don't do this. Not today."

"You still love him, don't you?" Shanice accused.

"What the fuck you talkin' 'bout?"

"My cousin. That's something he would say. He prolly told you that. You sound like him, and I hate that shit. I hate him."

"C'mon, baby. You trippin'. You mad 'cause you think I said somethin' you think he said. That don't make sense."

Shanice stood and spun around angrily. "So, now you callin' me crazy and stupid? Now I don't make sense?"

Queenie dropped her head, letting our a long, frustrated breath and rubbing her bald head. "I didn't say that. Stop puttin' words in my mouth. And stop overreacting to everything. I'm here with you because I wanna be. If I wanted to be wit' him, I would leave. Stop doin' this. You know I want you. How many times I gotta tell you that?"

Shanice crossed her arms over her naked breasts, the words going in one ear and out the other. "Do you still love him?"

Queenie let out a small laugh, shaking her head.

"See, that's what I'm talkin' 'bout!" Shanice accused. "I'm in love wit' you, but you still in love wit' him. Why? I don't understand. He left you in the streets to die. He don't care about you or love you like I do. I woulda never left you. You make sacrifices for love."

Queenie stood and got in Shanice's face. "Just like I'm making for you. You don't think I miss my sister? She prolly don't even know I'm alive. You ain't the only one makin' sacrifices, so don't tell me what love is. That's why I'm still here. Been here for two months. But if you can't handle this and keep questionin' me, then we don't have to do this."

Shanice's nostrils flared, eyes shrinking to angry slits. "Why you always gotta talk about leavin' every time we argue? That shit pisses me off."

"Because I don't wanna argue. I just want to chill and enjoy the time we have together. I almost died. You don't know what that feels like or how that can change you. I dream about dyin'. I don't wanna wake up to arguments about shit that don't matter. I'm here. With you. Take me as I am or leave me the fuck alone."

The women had an angry staring contest, gauging one another's level of ire, no one wanting to back down or give in. Both of their wills were strong, but Queenie's proved stronger.

"Okay," Shanice caved. "I'm sorry. I just love you so much, and I want all of your heart. My cousin–"

"Stop talkin' 'bout him!" Queenie snapped.

After another long stare, Shanice agreed. "Okay. I won't talk about him no more. It's me and you."

Queenie pulled her woman close for a kiss. "That's my girl. Now, don't you gotta get ready for work?"

"I do. What are you doin' today? You stayin' in?"

"Nah. I think I'ma get out and let Texas know I'm back."

"That's good. It's about time you left the house. You haven't been outside since you got here. Made me think you was runnin' from somethin."

Queenie frowned. "Gurl, you trippin'. I'm a Goddess. I don't run from nothin'. I just didn't know what I wanted to do. My mind needed healing, and bein' with you helped that. I almost died. That changed me in ways I can't even explain right now. All I know is I feel different. And I appreciate everything more. Like my time with you. I don't want to waste it arguing."

Shanice smiled like she had fallen in love all over again. "You can be sweet when you wanna be."

"And you can be bad when you wanna be. By the way, I like bad girls," Queenie smiled, palming Shanice's ass.

"Stop. I gotta shower and get ready for work and drop Shawntale off. Fuckin' wit you. I'ma be late. And what are you doin' today?"

"I been thinkin' 'bout gettin' in touch wit' a couple people."

"What that mean?" Shanice frowned. "I hope you not about to so somethin' that will get you in trouble. You just got shot. Why don't you sign up for school or get a job?"

Queenie smirked. "You know I ain't a nine-to-five bitch."

"But what about me and Shawntale? Those clubs ain't safe."

"Who said anything about a strip club? I ain't shakin' my ass for no more niggas. I had an epiphany while I was in the hospital. I don't wanna work for nobody again. I'm a Goddess."

***

Queenie stepped from the rented blue Toyota Rav4 with the grace of a ballet dancer. Her bald head shone in the Texas sun, the five pounds of missing hair making her feel lighter and brand new. Not having the dreads also brought out her facial features. Almond-shaped dark eyes, high cheekbones, and full, juicy lips.

If anything good came from being shot, it was the weight loss. Twenty pounds lighter and still curvy, Queenie walked up the sidewalk like she was on the runway at a fashion show. Tight fitting denim jeans flexed her new figure, making everyone she passed give her the 'damn' look. And the pink words across her tank top embodied how she felt: like a 'Bad Bitch!'

She stepped onto the porch of a blue and white house that looked a week from being condemned. After knocking on the door, she waited.

"Who is it?" a woman called.

"Queenie."

When the locks clicked and the door swung open, a bronze-skinned woman with long, curly black hair answered. Her eyes were hazel green, a button nose and thin lips giving her a baby face. But nothing about the beautiful woman was baby-like. Big breasts, a small waist, thick legs, and an ass that was made for clapping and twerking showed how blessed the woman was. On the scale of one to ten, she was an eleven.

When she seen Queenie standing on the front porch, her eyes popped, jaw dropping. "Girl, where yo' hair go!"

"Amber Rose ain't the only bitch that can do it. This a new me."

La'Qua stood there, eyes wide, mouth open.

"Is you gon' let me in or just keep starin' at me?"

The Latin beauty snapped out of her zone. "Damn, gurl. My bad. I wasn't expectin' you to come over lookin like' one of them bitches in *Black Panther*. And you lost weight, too. I'm jealous."

Queenie crossed her arms over her chest in an X. "Wakanda forever, bitch!"

After an embrace, Queenie was allowed in the house. Looking around, she couldn't hide her surprise at La'Qua's living conditions. The blue suede furniture was run-down, looking like it had been found curbside. Dirty clothes, empty food containers, and all kinds of junk was strewn across the living room. Roaches walked around lazily on the floor, wall, and ceiling, not bothering to hide from humans.

"Damn. You don't gotta look like that. I know our shit fucked up," La'Qua said, reading Queenie's face.

"I'm sorry. I just wasn't expecting…." Queenie's words trailed off as she looked around again.

"I know. This shit ain't what I want. Believe me. but I'm ridin' wit' my nigga. We gon' ball together and struggle together. Win, lose, or draw. Deso is my nigga."

"What happened to the house yo' granny left you?"

"Niggas found out where we lived and got at us. Damn near blew the house up. Turn out the house had $200,000 lien on it. The bank came wit' the sheriff and put us out. Deso an' 'em so hot that they can't get no money. Niggas even know who I am, so I can't hit the clubs. This all we can afford. And we might be about to lose this, too.

"Damn, baby girl. I didn't know y'all was down bad like this. Where Peso an' 'em at now?"

"Out trynna hit a lick. But they can't get close to no niggas wit' real money, so they been hittin' penny-ass sack boys. But enough about me. What's up wit' you, Princess, and Pop Somethin'? And why you was actin' all secretive, not wanting to talk on the phone?"

"Because you can't trust phones. That's how people get fucked over, talkin' too much. Save the important shit for face-to-face."

La'Qua was surprised by Queenie's serious tone. "Damn, bitch. Don't you think you takin' this Wakanda shit a li'l too far? Pop Somethin' rubbed off on yo' ass way too much. You seem different."

"If you almost died, it would change you, too."

La'Qua frowned. "Fuck you talkin' 'bout?"

"I almost died a couple months ago. I got shot four times."

La'Qua scoffed, looking Queenie from head to toe. "Stop playin', bitch. Show me the bullet holes. Yo' ass look fine."

Queenie reached for the bottom of the tank top, pulling it over her head. She didn't care about showing her naked breasts as she spun around to show off the wounds. One by her left shoulder blade, two in the center of her back, and one on her left rib cage.

"Oh, shit!" La'Qua cried, reaching out and touching the indentations. "Damn. When this happen?"

"A couple months ago."

"What Pop Somethin' and Princess say? They okay?"

"They left me in the middle of the streets, bleedin'."

Shock and surprise shown on La'Qua's face. Before she could get her words out, a key was inserted into the lock on the front door. Queenie barely had time to put her shirt on before Deso walked in the house, followed by Drama and Snot. They were talking about their latest move, but paused when they seen Queenie.

"Fuck she doin' here?" Drama mugged.

Snot made a move like he was reaching for a pistol. "I should pop yo' bitch-ass right now!"

"Y'all niggas chill," Deso spoke up, eyeing Queenie. "What up, shorty? Whatchu doin' here? How you find out where we live?"

"La'Qua told me. I need to talk to you, and she told me to come over."

Deso looked at his girl. "You couldn'ta called or texted me to let me know?"

La'Qua answered meekly. "She told me not to say nothin' 'cause of Drama and Snot."

"You don't owe that bitch no loyalty," Snot mugged. "She chose Pop Somethin' over us. Fuck that punk-ass bitch."

"I ain't gon' be too many more bitches, bitch-ass nigga!" Queenie mugged, poking out her chest.

Snot took a step forward, reaching out to grab her. Queenie stood her ground as Deso and La'Qua stepped between them.

"Chill, nigga!" Deso said, the irritation rising in his voice. "What's so important that you convinced my bitch to keep it a secret?"

Queenie stood tall, lifting her head, holding Deso's stare as an equal. "I want back in."

Deso looked to his girl to gauge her response to Queenie's comment. La'Qua looked surprised. Snot laughed.

"This some Nick Cannon wilin'-out shit?" Drama laughed.

Deso responded calmly. "Talk to me, Queenie. Last time I talked to Pop, y'all was up. Seein' a couple hunnit bands. You see how we livin'. We fucked up. What happened to Pop? I thought y'all was good?"

"We was." Queenie paused. "'Til they left me in the streets, bleedin'."

The explanation made Deso raise an eyebrow in wonder. "Fuck you talkin' 'bout?"

Queenie pulled off her shirt again, spinning around to show them her back. "Born Ready shot me in the back. Princess and Pop left me to die."

Deso's frown showed his disbelief. "They just left you? And what happened to Born Ready?"

"Pop killed him," Queenie said after pulling her shirt down. "And yeah, they left me. I don't know where they at. Pop didn't fuck wit' social media and didn't want me and Princess on it, either. I can't find them. And I don't want to."

"And you just expect us to let you back in?" Snot scoffed. "You put that nigga over us. You broke up the family. Fuck you."

"On the real," Drama added. "You a snake-ass bitch. Find yo' own way. We good."

"C'mon, y'all," La'Qua interjected, feeling sorry for her friend.

"She don't got nowhere to go. We can't do her like that."

"Why should we let you back on the team? Drama and Snot right. You left us," Deso said.

Queenie continued to hold her head high, seemingly unfazed by their lack of confidence in her. "First of all, this ain't 'bout Pop and my sister. I want a new start. And secondly, I don't wanna be a part of Pop Squad. I wanna be the leader."

"Fuck yo' ass been smokin'?" Deso laughed. "You just gon' show up at my house and try to take my spot after you been gone damn near a year?"

"The way I see it, y'all need me. Y'all fucked up and livin' in this raggedy-ass house and hidin' from er'body in Texas. I made connections. Y'all got the muscle and I got the knowledge. I seen a half mil, cash. Can't none of y'all say that. And if I got it once, I can do it again. Fuck this petty jack shit. It only cause problems. And I ain't trynna die over a chain that you niggas pawned for a couple hunnit. I wanna do it big. Almost dyin' changed my perspective on everything. I wanna live. See the world. Get a big-ass bag of money. But I need a team. I want y'all."

Drama laughed. "You gotta be shittin' me! Y'all hear this shit? Who she think she is? We know you, Queenie. Princess was yo' protector and backbone. Now all of a sudden you on some boss-ass shit 'cause you got shot up? I ain't goin'. Kick rocks."

"Keep talkin' shit and I'ma make you suck yo' own dick, gay-ass nigga. And I ain't no boss bitch. I'm a Goddess."

Drama turned to Deso. "Can I kill this bitch now?"

"Nah. Chill," Deso said. "This ain't the same Queenie we knew. Pop Somethin' told me about you before y'all left Texas. And now that you here, I see what he was talkin' 'bout. If you say you can get us up out this shit, then I'm in. Drama and Snot, if y'all don't like it, do y'all. But we fucked up right now, and she sound like she might be able to get us out this jam. I say we give her a shot. What else we got to lose?"

Queenie smiled, turning to look at Drama and Snot. "What y'all wanna do?"

Both men cut their eyes and looked away.

"You got yo' answer," Deso said. "So, what you wanna do?"

"First thing we gon' do is move outta Houston. When was the last time y'all was in Dallas?"

J-Blunt

Chapter 10

For the longest time it's been said that confidence makes a woman sexy. Queenie embodied both words, confidence and sexy, as she walked up to the front doors of Moonlight's Gentleman's Club. Two huge bouncers blocked her path, eyeing the bald beauty as she strolled up, ass bouncing and hips swaying to a tune that sounded like sex music. She wore light make-up consisting of dark eye shadow, gold bronzer, and dark purple lipstick to match the purple jumpsuit. Her gold heels clicked the concrete as she stopped before the awestruck bouncers.

"You don't work here, do you?" one of them asked, looking confused.

"Nah, but my friend does. What's the door charge?"

"Nothin' if I can see you dance later," the other man said, eyeing her from head to toe.

"Don't hold yo' breath." Queenie said, trailing a finger up his wrist, forearm, and bulging bicep.

A shiver went through the man's body as he opened the door, allowing her to pass free of charge. "That was a bad bitch!" he grimaced, watching her walk inside.

Moonlight's atmosphere was laid back compared to the places Queenie had danced. There was no ass-clapping contests or dope boys pouring liquor on strippers while making it rain. The music selection was a top forty songs. Ariana Grande's *God is a Woman* was playing smoothly from a sound system. Most of the clientele were white men. The dancers were mostly white women with a few Latin or light-skinned black women sprinkled in. Queenie counted one dark-skinned stripper wearing a blonde wig and blue eye contacts.

After parking her fatty on a barstool, she ordered a drink and watched the show on the main stage. A light-skinned woman with fiery red hair was topless, dancing like a sexy ballerina, doing tricks on the pole that made the men whistle and cheer. When her set was over, she collected the pile of money that had been thrown on the stage and disappeared.

After taking a sip of her drink, Queenie found and empty table and took a seat. Several women approached offering entertainment, but she denied them all. When the red-haired, light-skinned woman appeared again, Queenie waved her over. The woman recognized the bald-headed sex symbol instantly, her eyes growing wide as a full moon.

"Queenie! What the fuck you do to yo' hair?"

"I got a new look and a new attitude. You gon' gimme a hug or stand there witcho mouth open?"

After hugging like long-lost sisters, Skittlez took a step back and looked at Queenie again. "Damn, I can't believe you cut off all that hair. And you pullin' it off. Not too many hos can do that bald head. And it look like you lost weight."

"I did, I am, and I did. But forget about me. What the fuck you doin' in this stuffy-ass place wit' all these white people? I didn't know this was yo' crowd," Queenie said, noticing the bruises covering Skittlez left arm and wrist.

"It's a long story. Too long to tell right now. But what you doin' in here? I know you ain't come to be social or get a lap dance."

"No, this ain't a social call. I need to talk business."

Skittlez read the serious look in Queenie's eyes. "Okay. I get off in half an hour. Let me make a couple more rounds and then we can go. I gotta bleed these muthafuckas dry. You know how I do."

After sweet talking and lap dancing more money from the club-goers, the women walked out to the parking lot, stopping at Skittlez's E-class Benz.

"So, how the fuck you find me in this white-ass club? I thought y'all would be in Jamaica by now."

"You just like er'body else in the world that put they whole life on Facebook and Instagram," Queenie said, pausing. "And Jamaica is on hold. Indefinitely."

Skittlez read the reaction. "Did somethin' happen to Pop Somethin'?"

"Nah. Him and my sister left me. But that's not why I'm here. I'm here 'cause I want you on my team."

Skittlez laughed, looking in the sky at the half moon. "Gurl, you don't even know how much dram I got in my life right now. I know y'all bitches be gettin' a check, but I got too much on my plate."

Queenie was surprised by the denial. "It ain't like you to turn down an opportunity to run it up. Fuck goin' on?"

Skittlez let out a stressed breath, shaking her head. "Er'body got nightmares they hope don't come true or skeletons they hope to keep buried. Well, my nightmare is real."

Queenie placed a hand on her friend's shoulder. "You need help? What's goin' on?"

Skittlez sighed. "Four years ago I was fuckin' wit' a nigga that got locked up. I thought his ass wasn't gon' neva get back out. He used to beat my ass and had my self-esteem all fucked up. That's why I started stripping, 'cause it made me feel sexy and wanted. But that's a whole 'notha issue. Anyway, Monster is out. Got out right after y'all left and tracked my ass down. He don't want me at the hot spots 'cause he insecure. Want me around white people so I won't cheat."

Queenie got upset. "That's why them marks all over yo' arm? You lettin' a nigga put his hands on you?"

Tears threatened to spill from the light-skinned woman's eyes. "You don't understand, Queenie. His name is Monster for a reason."

"I don't give a fuck if his name was Jason or Freddy Kruger! Don't let no nigga control you or put his hands on you. Matter of fact, you not even goin' back to that nigga. You wit' me now."

Skittlez looked at Queenie like she had said the most ridiculous thing. "Didn't you just hear what I said? I can't get away from this nigga. Maybe if you was still wit' Pop Somethin' I would come with you. But two women ain't no match for him. He could kill us."

Queenie gave a dead stare. "You be surprised what I can do. And I ain't playin'. You not goin' back to this nigga. You on my team. I–" The ringtone on Skittlez's phone and look on her face made Queenie pause. "Is that him?"

Skittlez nodded, pulling out her phone. "Yeah. He callin' to see if I'm on my way home."

Queenie snatched the phone and answered it. "What?"

The man's voice was deep and powerful. "Who dis? Where my bitch at?"

"This Queenie. And yo' bitch just became my bitch. If you putcho hands on her again, I'ma cut cho dick off and make you suck it."

Monster's laugh sounded evil, making the hair on Queenie's neck crawl. "Okay, Queenie. Since you wanna play hero, tell her I'ma start wit' her li'l sister. I love virgin pussy. Bitch betta get her ass home right now. Ask her if I'm playin'."

Click.

Queenie removed the phone from her ear slowly, looking at it like it was a piece of space junk.

"What he say?" Skittlez asked worriedly.

"He said somethin' 'bout startin' wit' yo' li'l sister, and he love virgin pussy. Fuck is he talkin'–"

"Gimme my phone!" Skittlez shrieked, calling Monster back. "She was just playin', baby. That was my friend. I'm on my way home right now."

"Skittlez, what the fuck is that nigga talkin' 'bout?" Queenie asked.

Skittlez ignored Queenie, wiping the tears that rolled down her face as she unlocked her car door. "I'm sorry. I left my phone out and she answered it. I'm on my way right now. I'ma be there in twenty minutes." She hung up the phone.

"Skittlez, wait!" Queenie yelled, holding onto the door and stopping her from closing it.

Skittlez looked up with a kind of terror in her eyes Queenie had never seen. "What? I need you to leave me alone. You did enough. I gotta get home."

"What is he talkin' 'bout doin' to yo' sister? What kinda shit is you in wit' this nigga?"

"He gon' rape and kill her. That's what he do. My sister is only thirteen, Queenie. I can't let him touch her."

Queenie was shocked. That quickly turned into blazing rage.

"I'm not gon' let him touch you or her. I swear to God, I won't. I'ma follow you home."

"No, Queenie. You did enough. Just leave. I'm good."

***

Monster sat on the couch, light perspiration covering his pockmarked face. The fair-skinned man looked like a hybrid of human and great ape, head the size of a watermelon, small ears, a wide, flat nose, and lips that looked too big for his face. When the front door opened, his green eyes locked on the newcomer. "You late," he growled.

"I got pulled over for speeding. I got stopped by the police."

Monster rose from the couch slowly, taking his time walking over to Skittlez. He stood a massive six-foot-three, 320 pounds. Working out in prison gave his shoulders, chest, and arms intimidating definition, and the potbelly told of his love of food. "You seventeen minutes late. You said you was gon' be here in twenty minutes. It took you thirty-seven."

Skittlez cringed under the presence and stare of the enormous man. "I-I told you, I got–"

Slap!

The big man's massive hand was a blur, covering the entire left side of her face and head, sending her crashing into the wall. "Did I say you can speak, bitch? Don't talk unless I tell you to."

Skittlez instinctively tucked into the fetal position, covering her head, expecting to be beaten. Footsteps walking away made her lower her guard. Monster was heading toward the back of the house.

"Come in the room," he ordered.

Skittlez took her time getting up from the floor, checking her face for blood. Her hand was clean of blood, but the sting remained on the left side of her face. When she walked in the room, Monster was sitting on the bed.

"Why you hit me? You know they be trippin' when I go to work wit' bruises."

"Because you talked without permission. Like you doin' now. Shut up. Get naked."

Skittlez stood before him and undressed, waiting for him to tell her what to do next.

"Come here. Lift yo' leg."

Skittlez stood before him, placing one leg on the bed so her pussy was in his face. Monster leaned forward until his nose was touching her labia, then took a sniff.

"Did you fuck one of them crackers?"

"No. You know I didn't. Why we gotta go through this every night?"

"Because you a nasty bitch! I heard about you when I was locked up. Don't act like you wasn't trickin'. I'm makin' sure you ain't givin' my pussy away no more," he said before jabbing two fingers deep into her pussy.

"Uh!" Skittlez cringed as sharp pain went from her pussy to her brain.

"Don't act like you don't like that," Monster grinned, roughly shoving his fingers in and out.

Skittlez stood and endured the pain until it turned to pleasure. When his big lips found her pearl, she leaned her head back, reaching out and rubbing his bald head. Monster continued sucking and fingering her until she was on the verge of orgasm. Then his free hand shot up, wrapping around her throat, applying pressure, cutting off her air.

She withstood the pleasure and pain for as long as she could. When her face began turning blue, she grabbed ahold of his wrist, trying to get him to let her neck go. Instead of letting up, he squeezed harder. Skittlez lost consciousness, collapsing to the floor.

Monster let out an evil laugh before picking her up and throwing her on the bed. He positioned her so she was lying on her back, head hanging off the bed.

Her consciousness returned slowly as he undressed. Before she could become fully awake, the big man squatted down, forcing his dick into her mouth and fucking her face.

Skittlez choked, coughed, gagged, and slobbered as she

struggled to catch her breath and suck his dick. It took a few minutes, but she eventually got with the program. Then he began choking her again.

"Let her go!"

The strange voice in the house shocked Monster, making him pause. He looked behind him and seen the bald woman standing in the doorway. "Who the fuck is you?" he growled.

"I'm Skittlez's friend. We talked on the phone," Queenie said, not intimidated by the size of Monster or mug on his face.

The big man stood, spinning to face her. "How the fuck you get in my house? What you want?"

"The door was unlocked, so I let myself in. Let my friend go and leave her alone. She my bitch now."

Monster began laughing.

"Queenie, I told you to leave me alone," Skittlez said, terror in her voice and on her face. "Leave. I got it."

Queenie stood her ground. "Only way I'm leavin' is wit' you."

"She not comin' wit' you," Monster spoke up. "And this yo' last chance to get the fuck outta my house."

"Well, I guess I'ma have to make you let her go."

Monster laughed again, approaching her slowly, a dangerous look in his eyes. "And how you gon' do that? I'm a monster, bitch."

Queenie didn't shy away or shrink as the massive naked man got closer. She met the sadistic look in his eyes with a look that promised violence. "I ain't scared of monsters, nigga. Monsters scared of me."

One of his hands shot out, wrapping around Queenie's throat. He applied pressure as he lowered his face inches from hers. "Who is you that got monsters scared?"

"A Goddess," Queenie managed, dropping her purse to the floor. When the bag hit his foot, Monster looked down, feeling the cold steel press into his nuts. Surprise flashed in his eyes, and then fear. The smile that spread across Queenie's face told him he was fucked.

Pop!

"Ah, shit!" Monster roared, letting her go and grabbing his

dick.

The smell of fear, gunpowder, and singed fleshed got Queenie excited. She fired the .40 at Monster two more times, hitting him in the chest, sending the big man falling to the ground, blood pouring from his wounds. Queenie stood over him, watching his face and the look in his eyes. The monster was terrified. Scared of death and the Goddess of murder.

"Queenie, what the fuck!" Skittlez screamed, standing on the bed, eyes wide in panic.

"Look," Queenie said calmly, pointing at Monster. "He scared. Come watch him die."

"We gotta get the fuck outta here or we goin' to jail!" Skittlez continued hysterically. "Why did you shoot him? You didn't have to shoot him."

Queenie cut her eyes at Skittlez. "Listen to how you sound. This nasty-ass, sick-ass nigga was fuckin' yo' face while you was knocked out. And he was about to choke yo' ass out again. He beat yo' ass all the time, and he threatened to rape yo' li'l sister. His ass deserve to die. Now, quit actin' like a weak-ass bitch and come watch him take his last breath. He got off on makin' you suffer. Ain't no tellin' how many bitches he did this shit to. Now he can't hurt nobody else. Look."

Skittlez wrapped her arms around her breasts as she stepped off the bed and stood next to Queenie. Monster lay on the floor, struggling to breath, his chest moving up and down rapidly with a pained look on his face, the fear of death in his green eyes. Then the green in his irises seemed to fade, and the pained look on his face vanished.

Queenie exhaled a slow, satisfied breath, turning to Skittlez. "How that make you feel?"

Skittlez looked terrified, like she had seen a ghost. "Like a murderer. We need to get the fuck outta here. I didn't know you got down like this."

"I told you I wasn't gon' let this nigga keep puttin' his hands on you. You my bitch now. I'ma do whatever I gotta do to protect mine."

Skittlez frowned. "I'm yo' bitch? Girl, you trippin'. Can we just get the fuck outta here? What we gon' do wit' the body?"

Queenie stepped over Monster's body and began stripping. "First, I'ma need you to suck my pussy. Killin' niggas get me horny as fuck."

The red head looked flabbergasted. "Bitch, you done lost yo' damn mind? You just killed Monster. We gotta get the fuck outta here."

Queenie lay back on the bed, opening her legs wide. "Relax. Trust me. I got this. As soon as you make me cum, we gon' leave. Don't worry 'bout nothin' in this house. Best way to destroy evidence is wit' fire."

***

"I think I'm ready to tell my mother I'm with you."

Queenie looked up from the steak she was eating, locking eyes with Shanice. They were at their new house in a Dallas suburb, eating dinner at the kitchen table. The food had Queenie in a mouth-watering food heaven until Shanice's outburst. The confession had ruined her appetite.

"What's wrong with keepin' things the way they are? Don't nobody gotta know what we do. We grown. We live our lives doin' what makes us happy."

"But I don't want us to be a secret no more. I love you. My daughter loves you. I want us to be a family. Don't you want that, too?"

Queenie sat her fork down, thinking on her response. If she told how she really felt, an argument would ensue. And if she lied, she wouldn't be the goddess she claimed to be. "Shanice, I got love for you, but I think you movin' too fast. Let's enjoy each other's company and see where that leads."

The smile on Shanice's face faded, the whites inside her eyes blazing red, her brows furrowing. "What the fuck is that s'posed to mean? I thought we was together. That's what you said when I was bein' yo' nurse and tending the bullet wounds in yo' back. Now that you out runnin' the streets wit' yo' stripper bitches, you wanna change up?"

"C'mon, Shanice. It ain't like that. We are together. I just–"

"You just like all the other niggas I fucked with. Lie to get what you want, and then after you had it, you don't want it no more. You out all night and leavin' me in the house with Shawntale. Why you move me here if you was always gon' be gone? I don't know nobody in Dallas. I moved here for you."

"Stop puttin' words in my mouth. I didn't say I didn't wanna be with you. All I said was you movin' too fast. You talkin' 'bout a family and meetin' yo' momma and tellin' her we together. That's a lot."

"We live together and we fuckin'. Don't that make us family?"

Queenie was about to respond, but her phone rang. The caller name brought a pained look to her face.

Shanice crossed her arms over her chest, shooting daggers with her eyes. "I know you ain't about to answer that."

"It's important. Hold on." After pressing talk, she answered the call. "What?"

"You don't sound grateful at all for me savin' yo' life," a deep voice said.

"It ain't you, man. Now just ain't a good time. I'm goin' through some shit wit' my girl."

"Trouble in paradise?" He laughed. "Well, I'm 'bout to add to that, 'cause I got a problem with you, too. We made a deal, and I don't feel like you comin' through on yo' end. Yo' ass would be dead or in jail if it wasn't for me gettin' you out that hospital. It's been two months, and I still ain't got what I want. Tell me somethin', Queenie. Gimme a reason to feel like I shouldn't start turnin' up the heat."

"I can't find them. They haven't contacted nobody, and they don't do social media. I told you it will take time."

"Unfortunately, time ain't a luxury for you. You got a uncle that live in Houston, right? Uncle Larry?"

"I swear to God, if you touch my family–"

"I know you wasn't about to threaten me, was you?" he cut her off. "I don't like to be threatened. And you knew what you was gettin' into when I brought yo' ass back to life. I told you it would be consequences if you didn't get me what I wanted. You helped that nigga kill my brother. I don't give a fuck about yo' uncle or nobody else in yo' family. I will kill all them muthafuckas and put 'em all in the same grave. I want Pop Somethin', and I ain't playin' no games. Next time I call, you betta have somethin' for me or I'ma pay Uncle Larry a visit."

"Fuck!" Queenie cursed, sliding her phone across the table and lowering her head. She was in a jam. The lives of innocent family members were on the line. She struck a deal with the devil, and he wanted to collect in blood.

"You okay?" Shanice asked.

When Queenie lifted her head, a snarl had spread across her lips. "Do I look like I'm okay? I got real shit goin' on. People's lives are on the line, and all you wanna do is argue about bullshit. I don't got time for this," she said, grabbing her phone and heading for the front door.

"Wait, baby! I'm sorry," Shanice apologized, chasing Queenie and grabbing her by the arm.

Moving on instinct, Queenie snatched away, cocking her free arm back and slapping Shanice in the face. "Get the fuck off me, bitch! I don't got time for yo' shit."

As Queenie drove away, a tinge of guilt welled up inside her. She'd overreacted and put her hands on Shanice. She shouldn't have done it, but the emotional roller coaster was becoming too much. She had to let Shanice know who was in charge. She needed to bow down and respect Queenie's slot as the alpha woman in the relationship. And if she needed to be slapped every now and then to get the picture, then that's what it would be. But that problem appeared small compared to the lives of her family being in danger. She couldn't deal with this alone and needed to find Pop Somethin'.

"Damn, nigga. Where the fuck you at?"

***

"Damn, gurl. Why you look like you not here? Where you at and what's on yo' mind?" Skittlez asked as she parked the rented GMC truck in the hotel's parking lot.

Queenie shook her head from side to side. "It just feel like every time I take a step forward, somethin' always pushes me back. I'm tryin' to put us on, but to do it I gotta hurt feelings. Then, once I figure that out, somethin else comes out of nowhere and creates a whole 'notha problem."

"I don't know what you talkin' 'bout, and it don't seem like you wanna go into detail. Is you and Shanice havin' problems and I came along and made it worse?"

"Nah. I ain't got no problem with you. You exactly what I need."

Skittlez smiled. "That sound like so much game, but I ain't trippin'. After what you did for me, I would follow yo' ass to hell to have a threesome wit' the devil."

Queenie took the time to look deep into her eyes. "I'm not gon' lie to you, baby. That's one thing I won't do. But I'm not tellin' you everything. Just know and trust that I'm handling it."

Skittlez leaned over and pecked Queenie on the lips. "Good. And know that I got you. For real, for real. Whatever you need. Any time. Now, let's go get this money, bitch."

The women climbed from the SUV and went to find the hotel room of their next victim. After a few knocks, the door opened and ATM smiled a diamond-toothed smile. He was light-skinned, had a crisp-lined Philly fro, and wore a white wife beater and designer jeans. His eyes were low and red, and the goofy grin told the women he had already started the party.

"Damn! 'Bout time y'all badasses showed up. C'mon in. Where the other one at? I thought it was three of y'all."

"She gon' be a li'l late," Skittlez said.

"Even if she don't show, don't worry. We more than enough," Queenie flirted, rubbing his face and neck as they entered the room.

After closing and locking the door, ATM walked over to Skittlez and began grabbing ass and titties.

"Wait!" the temptress laughed, pushing him away. "Let us turn up wit' you first."

"Yeah, nigga. Chill," Queenie added. "We got this. We gon' make sure you get yours. Now, what you drinkin' and smokin'?"

ATM pointed to the bottle of 1738 Remy on the table. Next to it was a quarter pound of weed and a pack of blunt wraps. "My bad. I'm on some thirsty shit. My bad. But I popped a Viagra and y'all came in this bitch lookin' good as fuck. I'm ready to get crackin'."

"That one pill ain't gon' be enough for this pussy, nigga." Queenie teased, bending over and slapping herself on the ass.

ATM grabbed himself through his pants like his dick was hurting. "Damn, gurl! You can't be doin' a nigga like this. Hurry up and turn up so I can get my dick wet."

After pouring drinks and rolling a blunt, the women got high and entertained the man of the hour. ATM bounced around, not able to stay still as he watched the women kiss and feel each other's bodies. Then Skittlez forced Queenie onto her back and stripped her naked. After spreading her legs, she dove in face-first.

"Oh, shit! Damn, Skittlez!" Queenie encouraged.

When Queenie was good and wet, Skittlez went to the sex bag and pulled out a six inch vibrating dildo. She clicked it on and had Queenie get on her hands and knees. Queenie went wild as the vibrator went in her ass and she sat her pussy on Skittlez's face. The light-skinned vixen worked her magic on Queenie until a full-body orgasm had her moaning in pleasure and cum dripped from her pussy like she was peeing.

ATM stood and clapped his approval before emptying the money in his pockets on the bed. "Damn, y'all bitches sexier than a muthafucka! I can't take no more teasin'. Let me in!" he said, snatching off his tank top.

Before he could get his pants off, there was a knock on the door. "Who the fuck is that?" he cursed.

"That's our girl," Skittlez said. "Get the door."

The irritation on his face disappeared when he realized a third woman was about to be added to the sexy situation. Jadakiss' lyrics "Up in the Four Seasons havin' a foursome" flashed in his mind as he went to the door.

After checking the peephole and seeing La'Qua standing in the hallway looking fresh out of his dreams, his dick got harder. He was all smiles as he snatched the door open. "Dayum, girl! You–"

A gloved fist to the lips snapped ATM's head back, sending him stumbling into the wall. When he looked up again, Pop Squad was running into the room while La'Qua locked the door.

"Fuck is y'all? What y'all want?" ATM shrieked, checking his lips for blood.

"You know what dis is, nigga," Deso said, snatching him off the floor and shoving him onto the bed. "Tell us where that shit at."

"C'mon, mane. This all I got, is what's in the room."

Queenie addressed ATM while putting on her clothes. "Lie to us again and I'ma go kill yo' momma. We ain't no rookies, nigga. We did our homework. We followed you around the city for a week. That purple Cadillac you bought her is nice, but it ain't bulletproof."

ATM looked at Queenie in amazement, surprised they had followed him for so long without him knowing. Then he looked to Skittlez, cursing the day he'd met her at the strip club. Her pretty, light-skinned ass was his downfall. "A'ight. I got sixty bands and a half brick at the crib. My baby momma and shorty in there. Let me call so I can get them to leave. The safe in the bedroom closet. Code is 2018."

Drama shook his head and began laughing. "You mean to tell me we 'bout to get sixty racks and I didn't have to shoot nobody?"

"Power of the P-U-S-S-Y," La'Qua laughed, slapping Queenie on the ass.

"We gon' stay here wit' this nigga to make sure he ain't lyin'." Deso spoke up. "Y'all go get the money since nobody won't be payin' attention to three bitches goin' in."

"I was thinkin' the same thing. Y'all make sure he make that call and get them out the house," Queenie said as she slipped into her heels and took ATM's house keys. "Thanks for the money, baby. I wish you coulda got to taste my pussy. My shit is worth dyin' for."

Queenie, La'Qua, and Skittlez left the hotel in the truck, pulling up to ATM's house 20 minutes later. His girl was gone, and inside they found the safe exactly where he said it would be. After opening it and confirming the cash and dope, Queenie made the call to Deso.

"What up, baby? Tell me somethin' good."

"We got what we came for. Put that nigga to sleep."

Chapter 11

"So, after we get our money up, what's the plan? I don't wanna keep robbin' niggas. Ain't that how y'all burnt up Houston?"

Queenie blew out a cloud of smoke before reaching over to tap the blunt's ashes in the ashtray on the bedside table. She lay in bed with Skittlez in the back room of Pop Squad's new digs in a middle class neighborhood in Dallas. The three bedroom, one and a half bathroom Victorian-style house was a long way from the roach-infested shack in Houston.

"I got a plan. We just makin' these moves to get our money up, and then we on the move again. Hittin' these niggas is temporary. Ain't no real money in it, and it bring too much drama. I'ma find us a plug, and we gon' run it up."

Skittlez smiled, liking the sound of the plan. "Damn, yo' ass got it all figured out. That shit sexy, witcho bald-headed-ass."

"I'm just trynna make sure we don't ever go hungry. I learned a lot fuckin' wit' Pop Somethin'. One thing about that nigga was he made it happen by any means. I love that he never settled. He went out and took what he wanted. I wanna do the same. I don't ever wanna be out here fucked up."

A moment of silence passed between the women before Skittlez spoke. "You miss that nigga, don't you?"

Queenie took a long puff on the blunt before responding. "Every day."

"You don't know where they were heading? Y'all was leavin' Atlanta, right? Where was y'all goin'?"

"We talked about Florida, but I don't know if that's where they went. We never kept the same phone numbers or identities. We did so much that we had to constantly change it up."

"You don't think yo' sister looking for you?"

"I don't know. They prolly think I'm dead. I looked fucked."

"So, what happens to the plans you made wit' us if you catch back up with them?"

Queenie took her time thinking of a response. Before she could answer, Drama and Snot walked in the room wearing goofy grins.

"Pass that shit and make some room. I'm on my Jeezy shit. Let's smoke and fuck," Drama said, crawling onto the bed.

Snot was already stripping out of his knee-length cotton shorts. "Y'all heard my nigga. Bust that shit open."

"Wait, wait, wait!" Queenie protested. "I'm good. I ain't feeling it right now."

"C'mon, mane. You trippin'," Drama frowned. "How you gettin' new on niggas? You know how we do."

"Real shit," Snot added. "You ain't let niggas get in them guts since you been back. What kinda shit you on?"

Queenie slid out of bed, her mind already made up. Drama and Snot were her workers. She didn't want them to think anything more. She was no longer their bitch, but their boss. And she would fuck on her terms. Not theirs. "I'm good. Y'all go 'head and fuck Skittlez. I wanna watch."

"Damn, bitch. That's how you do me?" Skittlez frowned.

Queenie took a seat in the chair across from the bed. "These my niggas. Take care of that. We a team."

The horny goons didn't give her a chance to protest. Drama snatched off the sheet and Snot grabbed her legs, spreading them wide.

"Hold on!" Skittlez reacted. "Y'all ain't finna just start fuckin' me. One of you niggas betta eat my pussy and get it wet first."

"You gotta lick it before you stick it," Queenie laughed.

"You already down there, brah. Handle that," Drama said, standing on the bed, holding his dick near Skittlez's face.

"Man, this some weak-ass shit," Snot sulked, moving his face between Skittlez's legs.

The threesome kicked off with a bang, Drama standing over Skittles, one hand on the wall for balance as she attacked his dick. She slurped him hungrily, slurping on his tool like she was trying to get to the center of a tootsie pop. Drama closed his eyes, lifting his head toward the ceiling and guiding her head with his free hand. Even though Snot didn't want to eat her pussy, he gave his all. He sucked and licked Skittlez's clit, making the sex kitten moan and reach for the back of his head to pull his face deeper into the pussy.

Queenie felt powerful as she watched the *ménage à trois*. In her mind, they were her workers putting on a show for the boss, and it made her hornier than she'd ever been.

"A'ight, Drama, you fuck her from the back while Snot get head," Queenie instructed.

Skittlez knelt on all fours as the men switched positions. When Snot lay on the bed, the redhead went to work on his meat, returning the favor for giving her good head. Drama knelt behind Skittlez, admiring her round, light-skinned ass before spreading her cheeks apart and diving in. The young gunner didn't believe in taking it slow and steady. Instead, he drilled her pussy like it was the last fuck before going off for a long prison sentence.

Skittlez took the D like a champ, throwing her ass back at Drama while continuing to give Snot bomb-ass head. Queenie was so turned on by the voyeurism that her hands developed a mind of their own. One hand found its way to her clit while the other rubbed and squeezed her nipples.

When she tired of the train, she gave more instructions. "A'ight. Change it up again."

"Wait. Hold on," Drama panted, on the verge of busting.

"Let us do this," Snot added. "Her head game is up top, and she gotta drain this muthafucka."

Queenie got irritated by the backtalk. "Skittlez is my bitch. Y'all fuck her how I say or don't fuck her at all."

Drama stopped mid-stroke, mugging Queenie. "Chill wit' the power trip. Fuck you think you talkin' to?"

Queenie looked at Skittlez. "Get up. Let them niggas get blue balls."

The light-skinned woman's reaction was immediate. She stopped sucking Snot and crawled away from Drama.

"What kinda shit is that?" Snot asked, looking back and forth from Queenie to Skittlez.

"She my bitch," Skittlez said obediently.

"Fuck her how I say or y'all ain't gettin' no pussy," Queenie repeated.

"Mane, you on some real fuck-shit," Drama mugged. "You

lucky she got some good pussy. What we doin'?"

"One in the ass and one in the pussy."

"Oh, hell nah!" Skittlez protested. "Ain't no nigga stickin' his dick in my ass."

"They is today," Queenie said matter-of-factly. "Get on top of Snot. Drama, get behind her and fuck her in the ass. Go slow. She a virgin."

Drama eyed Skittlez's ass like it was a game show prize. "You heard the boss."

After giving Queenie a long look, Skittlez climbed on top of Snot, slipping his dick in her pussy, waiting for Drama to go in her ass.

"Use yo' finger to get it loose," Queenie said.

Drama sucked his finger and slipped it into her ass.

"Oh, shit!" Skittlez moaned, tightening her sphincter as Drama worked his finger in and out. After a few moments, she relaxed, liking the feel of the finger as she began riding Snot. "Damn, boy. That shit feel good."

When her hole was wet and ready, Drama inched his dick into her anal walls. It took a while, but he eventually got it all in, squatting over her froggy-style as she rode Snot.

"Oh. My. God. Queenie. This. Shit. Feels. Too. Good," Skittlez moaned, loving the double penetration.

Queenie wiggled her finger on her clit at lightning speed, loving the D.P. show.

"Damn! Y'all in here gettin' it on!" La'Qua said, showing up in the doorway.

The threesome participants didn't even acknowledge her presence.

"Them muthafuckas ain't playin'," Queenie managed, not taking her eyes off the sex show.

"I came in here for you. We need to talk. It's important," La'Qua said, her tone serious.

The tone of her friend's voice took away Queenie's lust. "Why you sound so serious? What up?"

"Can you come to Houston wit' me so I can see my daughter?

They granting visitation this weekend, and Deso don't wanna step foot in Houston. He think somebody might see him wit' us and try to sweat us while we visiting her. If some shit like that happen, we ain't gon' never get her back."

"Damn, La'Qua. Why you gotta come with that serious-ass shit while they fuckin'?" Queenie sulked.

"My bad. I did fuck up the mood, huh? But don't trip. I can help you get it back."

Without being told, the Latin bombshell knelt between Queenie's legs and began eating her pussy. Sex music filled the room as everyone got their morning rocks off.

Deso walked in the room, surprised by the orgy. "Damn. That's how y'all leave a nigga out the loop?"

La'Qua stopped eating Queenie to look up at her man. "All you gotta do is get behind me."

"I am. But first I gotta break up the party. Queenie, somebody at the door for you."

"Who is it?" Queenie asked, irritation in her voice. She wanted to bust a nut and was tired of the interruptions.

"It's Pop's li'l cousin, Shanice."

Surprise spread across her face and through her body, killing the vibe. "Where she at?"

"In the living room," he answered, noticing the change in her mood. "You good?"

None of Pop Squad knew of the lesbian relationship, and now wasn't the time to tell them. And then there was Shanice. She had no idea how the love-struck woman had tracked her down, nor did she like being tracked down. She hadn't gone home for a reason, but it seemed Shanice wouldn't learn her lesson. It was time to teach her another one.

"Yeah. We good. Tell her to come back here."

Deso studied Queenie for a moment. "You serious? You want her in here?"

Queenie grabbed La'Qua's head and moved it toward her pussy. "Yeah. She need to see this."

After one last look, Deso disappeared from the room. Queenie lay back, a smile spreading across her lips as La'Qua went to work.

An audible gasp made everyone stop what they were doing and look toward the door. Shanice stood there, eyes wide with anger and hurt. For a moment Queenie regretted allowing Shanice to see La'Qua eating her.

The remorse was short-lived when she heard the scream and felt a sharp pain sting her ear. "Bitch!" Shanice yelled, punching Queenie on the side of the head and diving on top of her. The chair tipped over and the women fell to the ground, Shanice on top. She was able to deliver two more punches to Queenie's face before Deso grabbed her.

"What the fuck you doin'? Chill!"

"Let me go, Deso! Let me go!" Shanice screamed, trying to wrestle out of the bear hug.

Drama, Snot, and Skittlez stopped their threesome to watch the violence as Queenie jumped up from the floor with a mug on her face and the desire for vengeance in her eyes. She attacked Shanice like they were enemies, throwing rights and lefts.

La'Qua eventually grabbed her, but not before she did damage to Shanice's face. "Fuck y'all fightin' for?" La'Qua asked, unsure what to do.

"Let me go, Qua! Let me go!" Queenie yelled, wanting some more.

"Don't let her go!" Deso said, struggling to hold Shanice. "Y'all muthafuckas chill! Fuck y'all fightin' for?"

Shanice ignored the question, screaming at Queenie, "You wanna play wit' me, bitch? I'ma beatcho ass. Let me go, Deso!"

"You the one actin' immature and insecure, bitch. I got hands, don't I? Put blood in yo' mouth, ho?" Queenie screamed, also struggling to get free.

And then she got loose, rushing Shanice. Anticipating the move, Shanice used the bear hug Deso had her wrapped in for leverage, leaping in the air and kicking Queenie in the chest. Queenie flew in one direction while Deso and Shanice crashed into the wall, falling to the ground.

Like martial arts fighters in an action movie, both women were on their feet quickly, charging one another, fists flying. Several punches were exchanged as the lovers stood toe-to-toe and boxed until Queenie threw a punch that caught her girl square on the chin.

Shanice's head snapped back as she lost her footing, dropping to her knees. The fight was over.

"Damn! On what, they wasn't just thumpin'!" Drama yelled, excited by the fight.

Snot jumped off the bed and stood over Shanice, imitating Smokey on the ghetto classic *Friday*. "Damn, Shanice! You just got knocked the fuck out!"

Nobody laughed except Drama and Snot.

"Y'all good now?" Deso asked, looking back and forth from the fighters. "Fuck y'all fightin' for?"

Queenie touched a hand to her face, checking for blood. Red fluid on her fingers confirmed a busted lip and nose. "Yeah. We good. She know what's up. Y'all get out. Give us a minute."

Deso looked at Queenie, questioning her intent. "Y'all ain't finna box no more, is y'all? 'Cause if y'all is, I want front-row."

Queenie shot him a mug. "Get out."

When Pop Squad left the room, Shanice got up from her knees, checking her face as she sat on the bed. Her eye was swelling, along with her bottom lip. "That's how you do? Gon' disrespect me like that?"

"I wasn't disrespectin' you."

Shanice looked at Queenie like she wanted to fight again. "What the fuck you call lettin' anotha bitch lick yo' pussy when you know I'm 'bout to walk in the room?"

"I was trynna bust a nut and teach yo' ass a lesson."

Shanice walked up on Queenie.

"Betta stop 'fore I knock yo' ass out again!" Queenie threatened, cocking an arm back.

"That was a lucky punch, bitch. I was beatin' yo' ass. And I ain't finna fight you no more. I just wanted you to look me in my eyes and explain this bullshit. What lesson was I s'posed to learn from this? That you don't love me?"

"Nah. That I'ma do what I want and all the bullshit you doin' is drivin' us apart. You trynna play family, and I'm trynna get money. I ain't trynna settle down and get married. I trynna eat and make a way for my team. And this how we move. I was Pop Squad before I met you or Pop Somethin'. These my niggas. We all fucked each other and ate off the same plate. As a team. This what I come from. This where I wanna be."

Shanice looked devastated. "So, this is it? What about us?"

"It's up to you. But this my team. They move how I move. I'm not leavin' them for you. We trynna get it up. I need them."

"You ain't shit, you know that?" Shanice cursed, blinking away the tears that threatened to spill. "You ain't no better than none of the niggas I fucked wit'. Fuck you!"

"Don't fuck me. Fuck wit' me. I treated you better than all the niggas you ever fucked. I never lied to you. I'm tellin' you what it is. The rest is up to you."

"I said what I had to say. Fuck you, bitch."

"Then why you still standin' in my room? In my house?" Queenie asked.

Shanice could no longer hold back the tears. "Because I love you, bitch. And you hurt me. And I wanna leave, but I can't."

Queenie moved for the door. "Well, I'ma make it easy. I'ma leave."

"Wait!" Shanice shrieked, sounding like a drowning woman about to miss her rescue.

Queenie paused. "What?"

Shanice broke down. "Don't do this to me, Queenie. Please. I love you, baby, and I need you. I'ma be a better girl. I promise. I just wanna be with you."

It took all Queenie's will to hold back the smile that threatened to spread across her face. She couldn't believe Shanice had caved. And if she could have her cake and eat it, too…. "This my team, Shanice. We take care of each other on every level. Even fucking. If you can't handle this, leave."

Shanice put on her bravest face, the knot above her eye steadily growing. "I'm not leaving. I can handle it. I swear to God, I can."

Queenie eyed her for a moment, looking for a sign of her being unsure. "If you say so. Okay. So, tell me how the fuck you found me."

"I followed you here a couple weeks ago. I knew about this house for awhile. I just didn't know what was goin' on in here."

Queenie shook her head, giving Shanice a look. "You a real bitch for following me. But okay. I need you to go back home and let me settle everything with the team. They didn't know you was my girl."

Shanice got defiant. "I told you I wasn't leavin'. I'm stayin' with you. I wanna be part of the team."

Queenie laughed. "You trippin'. You got a daughter. You ain't finna bring her into this."

"I took her to Houston yesterday. She wit' my momma."

The news surprised Queenie. "So, you just gon' leave her?"

"Like you said, she can't be here. She safer wit' my momma."

"And you sure this what you wanna do? You gon' leave Shawntale and just drop her off?"

"I need to do this for me. I don't know how I'ma feel about it tomorrow or the next day, but this is where I wanna be. I wanna be part of the team."

Queenie looked at Shanice, a challenge in her eyes. "Okay. Prove it."

Shanice met and held her stare. "What you want me to do?"

Queenie looked toward the door. "Drama and Snot! C'mere!"

J-Blunt

Chapter 12

X-Scape wasn't much to look at in the daylight hours. Right on the outskirts of downtown Dallas, the 2400-square-foot building was almost invisible. Plain gray bricks and a thick, dark-tinted picture window made up the structure. On the wall was the club's named spelled horizontally in block letters.

At night the bland building was transformed into a hustler's gathering spot where they showed off their hard-earned dough, and tonight was no different. Foreign whips on chrome and donks with wet paint jobs filled the parking lot. The party-goers who couldn't get in the club turned the lot into their own hot spot while the big boys showed out indoors. Expensive bottles flooded all the tables in the VIP as the ballers partied.

Amongst the VIPs were four of the most dangerous women in Texas. Queenie flexed her curves in a black mini-dress and gold heels. The skin-tight 'freak 'em dress' showed her slimmed-down figure, her ass and titties on full display. When she walked by, niggas and bitches loved and hated to see the bald-headed bad bitch.

Next to her, Shanice stood sipping a glass of Moscato, looking flawless. She had dropped the good girl image, rocking a sheer pink dress that left nothing to the imagination. The fringe at the bottom barely covered her voluptuous ass cheeks, and her Double-D breasts and nipples were on full display in the almost see-through fabric.

Not to be outdone, La'Qua stunted on every female who hadn't come to the club on fleek. Luscious black hair flowed past her shoulders. The green print dress with a plunging neckline showed off a body that made people's mouths water if they looked at her too long.

And finally, Skittlez wore a tight purple dress, showing everybody she was the best thing smoking since purple haze hit the hood. She danced freely, shaking all of her jiggley parts to the bass-pounding music.

TK was the unofficial leader of Fly Boys Love Haters, "Fly Boys" for short. Short and slim with a wiry build, the light-skinned pretty-boy was easy for the women to latch onto. Loud with a reckless mouth and look-at-me attitude, he didn't question that the four bad bitches were only interested in him.

"When the Fly Boys come out, you see how we set the city off!" TK bragged, dancing with Skittlez, hands all over her body parts. "Ain't no party like a Fly Boy party, 'cause a Fly Boy party go hard!"

"I can't wait to see the after-party!" Skittlez smiled, grabbing TK's dick.

"You keep grabbin' that muthafucka and he gon' bite cho ass!"

Skittlez licked her lips. "Don't threaten me wit' a good time, nigga. I bite back."

Queenie slipped up behind TK, grabbing him around the waist as the women sandwiched him. "I heard y'all talkin' 'bout a good time. If it ain't no party like a Fly Boy party, then it ain't no good time if the queen ain't involved."

"Y'all betta quit touchin' me like that 'fore I shut it down early. I can handle more than one of y'all."

"But can you handle three?" La'Qua said, walking over and grabbing Queenie and Skittlez's asses.

"Damn, my nigga. Caring is sharing," Rock Star laughed, wanting in on the party. "Send some of that honey love my way. You can't handle all that, li'l nigga."

TK smiled at his longtime friend. "I'm a boss, nigga! Fly Boy Ten Karat do ten in a row. My California king built for more than one or two."

"Fly nigga shit!" Rock Star saluted, dipping off to find himself somethin' to smash for the night.

"So y'all fuckin' wit' a nigga or what? No game playin'. I wanna see if y'all for real 'bout this orgy. I ain't playin' no games."

Queenie slipped a hand in TK's pocket, grabbing his piece. "This only for one night, nigga. Me and my girls just wanna play around for the night, and you seem like the only nigga in here that can back up his word. This night gon' change yo' life."

Lust and the promise of a good time shown on TK's face."

"Fuck we still doin' standin' here? Let me grab a couple of my niggas and we bailin'."

"Nah, baby," La'Qua said. "This night is for you only."

TK looked amused. "Y'all bullshittin', right? My niggas come wit' me er'where I go. Fly Boys move in a flock like birds. That's how we stay safe. Hold on. I'ma be right back."

When TK walked away, Shanice panicked. "We not doin' this still, is we? It's too many of 'em. What if we can't get him by his self?"

"Quit, buggin', baby girl. We got this." Queenie said, trying to calm her.

"I'ma text Deso an' 'em and tell 'em to fall back." La'Qua said, pulling out her phone.

TK headed back toward the women wearing the smile of a man who just hit the jackpot. "I hope y'all ready to spend the night wit' the flyest nigga God created."

***

Drama coasted the Jeep Cherokee along the highway, making sure to obey all speed limits and traffic laws. In the passenger seat was Deso. Snot was in the back. All of them were armed with semi-automatic weapons and extra clips.

"Queenie trippin', tellin' us to hold up," Snot vented. "We can't let $200,000 get away like that. I'll kill the nigga whole team for two hunnit Gs."

"We just seein' the lay of the land," Deso spoke, trying to keep his gunners cool. "Ain't no need to hit 'em right now if we find out where they kick it at."

"But if the opportunity present itself, we gotta make the grab. I'm wit' Snot. For two hunnit bandz, all them niggas'll get it," Drama said. "It's seven of them and seven of us, countin' the bitches. Wit' the element of surprise, we can knock all them niggas down.

"Queenie called it off. We just takin' a look," Deso said. "And don't get too much closer. We followed these niggas for twenty minutes and they ain't seen us yet. Don't get sloppy."

The irritation reflected in Drama's voice. "I know how to

follow a nigga. And how you lettin' Queenie call the shots now? Just 'cause that bitch bagged some niggas and got shot up, that's s'posed to make her a Made Man or somethin'? That bitch betrayed us wit' Pop bitch-ass. Ain't no way she can come back and get top dawg status."

"What he sayin', up top," Snot added, eyeing Deso. "She shouldn't be callin' shit, my nigga. Only reason I agreed is 'cause you agreed, and I fuck witchu the long way."

Deso raised his voice a notch. "You niggas gotta get over that old shit. She moved on wit' my nigga and got it up. Now she back trynna help us get it up. She got connects. Fuck who callin' the shots, long as niggas ain't broke. That's what matter. Y'all gotta get over that bullshit and accept her back. She Pop Squad, and she official."

The SUV grew silent as they digested Deso's words.

"Yeah. I hear you," Drama spoke up. "But I still feel how I feel. And if we get the opportunity, I think we should make the move on these niggas."

"Me too," Snot agreed.

Pop Squad continuing following the Fly Boy entourage from the highway, down some back roads, and into the rear parking lot of a music studio. A blanket of darkness covered the area, making the jack boys' faces light up.

"It don't get no betta than this!" Snot said excitedly.

Drama looked around in all directions. "I don't see no cameras or witnesses. Let's dump these niggas and take TK bitch-ass. Let's get it!"

Deso was undecided. He wanted to fall back like Queenie said, but this opportunity seemed too good to pass up. If they stormed the Fly Boys, they could easily kill half of them before they could get off a shot. Queenie and La'Qua were strapped and already in the Benz with TK. Everything seemed perfect. Almost too perfect.

"What we gon' do?" Snot asked, excitement in his voice.

Deso made up his mind. "Let's go get this money!"

***

122

A light wind blew across the dark parking lot, sending a hamburger wrapper tumbling across the pavement. Queenie's eyes darted around the darkness as she clutched her purse tightly. Something wasn't right. She could feel violence in the air, making her skin tingle and nipples get hard. Pop Squad was close by. She could feel them. The dark parking lot was the perfect place to set up an ambush.

"This the same studio that made Li'l Flip and Beyoncé famous," TK bragged as he shuffled the women from the car. "My nigga, Li'l Boog, got next. Make sure y'all check him out on YouTube and SoundCloud. Matter fact, I might need y'all in the next video. Put ch'all on the map."

"Hey, I definitely need to put this ass on TV!" La'Qua sang, stopping to twerk for the Fly Boy crew.

While the money-getters stopped to admire the Latino woman's fatty, Pop Squad made their move. Deso led the charge, firing a Drako as he emerged from behind the building.

D-Nice was the first Fly Boy to fall, taking bullets to the face, neck, and chest. Before the Fly Boy hit the ground, Drama followed his mentor into battle, the AK-47 lighting up the night as chopper bullets tore into a Suburban parked in front of TK's Benz. Snot followed in the rear with an MP5, wanting to get a clear shot so he could put the fully automatic to work.

He got his wish when the Fly Boys pulled pistols and began shooting back. Fly Boy's M.A. hadn't fully cleared the side of the suburban before he upped his pistol. He had a clear shot at Drama as the Pop Squad member sprayed chopper bullets wildly. M.A. locked onto the jack boy, about to squeeze the trigger. That's when Snot's MP5 erupted, making M.A.'s body shake as hot lead lit him up.

TK ducked behind his Benz, pulling the 9mm Taurus from his waist. He looked around to see where his niggas were and who had heat. Darez, Wako, and Tru already had their heats out, trying to find who was shooting at them. When he looked at the women, TK was surprised they weren't screaming and crying. Instead, they crouched down a few feet away, watching him intently. Being the perfect showman, Fly Boy Ten Karat rose up and joined the firefight.

For the first time since waking up from being shot, Queenie was unsure what to do. Pop Squad hadn't listened. She was pissed. The hot boys had put all their lives in danger. The way she figured, she had three options: join her niggas in the shootout to kill everybody and try to take TK alive, wait it out to see what happened, or make a run for it.

After making her decision, she could feel eyes on her as she pulled the 380 Glock from her purse.

When Fly Boy Ten Karat seen Queenie pull the pistol from her purse, he had an epiphany. It was a set-up. That's why all the women chose him. That's why they wanted to get him alone. That's why they weren't hysterical during the shooting. And that's why she had a pistol.

Before she could aim it, TK turned his pistol on her. Queenie watched the realization dawn in his eyes and knew she wouldn't be able to shoot him before he shot her. The only thing she could hope was to hit him on the way down.

Clap, clap, clap! TK's pistol barked.

Skittlez seen it all unfold and dove in front of Queenie, taking the bullets meant for the black beauty. She fell on top of Queenie, shielding her from TK's blazing death. Queenie fired back, unable to get a clean shot because Skittlez was on top of her. The only thing she succeeded in doing was sending him running.

After crawling from under her girl, Queenie checked the damage. Two holes in her chest leaked life fluid as the woman struggled to breathe. "Damn, bitch! Why the fuck you jump in front of me?" Queenie asked, grateful to be alive, but sad her girl got shot.

"I-I c-couldn't–" Skittlez tried to speak, but ended up coughing up blood.

"Don't talk. Save yo' strength," Queenie said, applying pressure to the holes in her chest to try to stop the bleeding. "La'Qua, get one of them cars! We gotta get outta here!"

La'Qua kept low, bullets whistling over her head and clanking into vehicles as she looked inside for a set of keys. "I got one!"

Queenie turned and seen La'Qua climbing into a Benz truck. Refusing to leave Skittlez, she turned to Shanice for help. The newbie was frozen stiff, eyes wide, scared for her life. "Snap out of that shit, bitch, and help me get her to the truck!"

Shanice's eyes cleared like she had awoken from a bad dream, then she jumped into action, grabbing Skittlez's feet as Queenie grabbed her arms.

They kept low, carrying her to the truck. "We gotta get her to the hospital!" Queenie screamed, covered in blood as she tried to stop Skittlez's bleeding.

"She ain't gon' make it," La'Qua said somberly.

"You ain't no doctor, bitch. Just get to the hospital. We gotta try to save her." Shanice sat in the front seat with wide eyes, listening to Skittlez's death moans and watching the life drain from her body. The sight, sounds, and smell of blood chilled her to the bone, making her shiver.

"C'mon, Skittlez! Don't die on me. You bet not die on me, bitch!" Queenie said, slapping her across the face.

Skittlez mumbled something unintelligible and spat out more blood. Death was moments away, and no one could stop it.

And then it came, the life slowly draining from her eyes as her face went slack.

"Skittlez! Skittlez!" Queenie screamed, slapping her again.

"She gone," La'Qua spoke up, watching Queenie through the rearview mirror.

Queenie closed her eyes, shoulders slumping as she let out a long breath.

"Where we goin'? What we gon' do wit' her?" La'Qua asked.

When Queenie opened her eyes, they burned with anger. "Call Drama an' 'em bitch-asses. This they fault. They got my bitch killed."

***

When the Jeep pulled up behind the Benz truck, Queenie bounced out of the back seat covered in Skittlez's blood, 380 in her fist. Deso shrank back, a little unnerved by the sight of the blood.

"You a'ight?"

"Hell nah! You stupid-ass niggas got Skittlez killed. I told y'all dumbasses to fall back. Why the fuck didn't y'all listen?"

Shock spread across Deso's face. Then fear. "Skittlez dead? Where La'Qua?" he asked, moving to look in the truck. Skittlez lay across the back seat, La'Qua and Shanice up front. "You good, baby?"

"We told y'all to fall back!" La'Qua yelled, her eyes brimming with tears. "Y'all coulda got us all killed."

Devastation and guilt spread through Deso. "Damn, baby. We fucked up. My bad."

"That shit ain't gon' bring Skittlez back!" Queenie snapped. "I told y'all bitch-asses to fall back. This my team. These my–"

"Betta watch yo' mouf, Queenie!" Deso mugged. "I don't give a fuck 'bout you bein' mad. You ain't gon' talk to me like that."

The alpha male and alpha female had a stare down. Queenie knew what Deso was capable of. He wasn't a flunky like Drama and Snot. He was groomed by Pop Somethin'. And although he wasn't imposing and could be reasonable at times, he still wasn't to be fucked with. As bad as she wanted to teach him a lesson, she knew she couldn't. Deso controlled Drama, Snot, and La'Qua, and she needed them all right now.

So she piped down, her voice losing some of the edge. "Y'all fucked up, Deso. For real. Skittlez had all the info. She knew all the big boys in Dallas. Our plans is fucked. That's why I'm so pissed. Y'all bogus."

Deso calmed a little. "I didn't mean for it to happen like that. We had an opportunity and tried it. I thought y'all could grab the nigga while we kept his boys busy."

While Queenie and Deso went back and forth, Snot and Drama got out the Jeep to see what was going on. "What happened?" Drama asked.

"Skittlez dead," Queenie said aggressively, "and it's y'all fault.

Y'all got the only person wit' the info we need killed. Good job, niggas."

"We tried to make a move," Snot explained. "We thought y'all was gon' be ready."

"We wasn't. And I told y'all asses to fall back. Next time I say don't do nothin', don't do it!"

Drama sucked his teeth. "Betta calm yo' ass down. You ain't talkin' to no fuck-boys."

Queenie mugged him, the promise of retribution in her eyes. "Do some more stupid-ass shit and see what happen."

J-Blunt

Chapter 13

Queenie lay in bed, staring at the ceiling, mind on overdrive as thoughts raced by so fast she couldn't focus. They were so close to the come-up. So close to getting a bag. And it disappeared like a rock in a crack pipe because of their stupid-ass, trigger-happy niggas. She was questioning her decision to get back with the gang. They had already burned up one city because of their stupidity, and now they appeared to be doing the same thing in Dallas. She wished she could be back with Pop Somethin' and her sister instead of locked in a partnership with a bunch of fools who might get her killed.

The vibrating of her phone pulled her from the rumbling thoughts. Uncle Larry's name shown on the screen. A flash of excitement passed through Queenie. She hadn't heard from him in a while, and she was hoping he was calling with news about Princess. "Hey, Uncle Larry!"

"This ain't cho uncle."

A chill raced through her body when she recognized the voice. "Fuck you doin' wi' my uncle phone? Where he at?"

"The more important question is where Pop Somethin' and yo' sister at? Tell me somethin', Queenie."

"C'mon, D.D., I told you last time I haven't found them yet. I'm tryin'. They low. I need more time," she pleaded, hoping to get her uncle out of trouble.

"You outta time. And so is yo' uncle. I told you I didn't play, bitch. Mr. Bill Collector came to collect. Say bye."

"D.D., wait! D.D.?" Queenie screamed.

"What's goin' on?" Shanice awoke.

"Q-Queenie? This you, baby girl?" Uncle Larry asked, sounding weak.

When Queenie heard the pain in his voice, something inside her broke, bringing the tears. "Yeah, uncle. You okay?"

"Nah, li'l one. Yo' boys in my house, and I think they 'bout to kill me. I seen all they faces, and they askin' 'bout yo' sister and some nigga named Pop Somethin'. I don't know–"

Pow!

Queenie flinched at the gunshot, her eyes wide as fear gripped her body. "Uncle Larry! Uncle Larry!"

"I told you his time was up," D.D. said. "And so is yours. I I'm not leavin' Texas 'til I bury yo' ass."

Click.

Tears ran down Queenie's face as she stared at the phone. Her uncle was dead. It was her fault. She made a deal, unknowingly trading his life to save her own. She wished she could go back and remake the deal. For the second time in two days, death had taken someone close to her.

"What happened, baby?" Shanice asked, concern in her voice.

"My uncle. He dead," Queenie cried.

"Oh, baby!" Shanice lamented, pulling Queenie close and wrapping her in an embrace. "What happened? Was he sick? Why was you screamin'?"

Queenie didn't respond right away. She drowned herself in the warmth and love of Shanice's arms as she mourned her uncle and Skittlez. When she was ready, she opened up. "Some niggas that's lookin' for me, Pop, and my sister killed my uncle."

Horror shown on Shanice's face. "What happened?"

"While we was in Atlanta, we got to fuckin' wit' these SOD niggas and tried to take over the city. That got us in some shit with these other niggas that call theyself Grind Squad. Turns out Grind Squad plugged in other states, but we didn't give a fuck. We hit them niggas and killed the leader, D.D.'s brother. Then we fell out with the SOD niggas we was plugged with and moved on. Pop killed this nigga Born Ready brother, and he found out right when we was about to leave. He the one that shot me. Then D.D. kidnapped me from the hospital and we made an agreement for my life, in exchange I bring him Pop Somethin'. But I can't find Pop, and now D.D. killin' my family members until he can get me or Pop."

As Shanice listened to the story, her face reflected the range of emotions she experienced. The lasting one was anger. "Why didn't you tell me this earlier? What the fuck he get you into?"

"I was trynna work it all out. I thought I would be able to catch back up wit' Pop before D.D. came to collect. Plus, I didn't want you to get involved. I got a lotta baggage."

"But I've accepted everything else. And I accept this, too. We gotta find him."

"Who?"

"Pop Somethin'. Everywhere he go, he make it bad for everybody, but he always find a way to make it out unhurt. You should've told me this before. So, all we gotta do is give him Pop and he gon' leave you alone?"

"That's what he said. But that wasn't my plan. When I find Pop, I'm not tellin' D.D. where he at."

Shanice looked confused. "Why not? If he wants Pop Somethin' give him what he wants so you can live. You said he plugged, right? That means you gon' be marked."

"It's not that easy, baby girl. I'm not C-Note. I'm not turnin' on my nigga. When I find Pop, we gon bring it to D.D. and Grind Squad."

Jealously, hurt, and anger shown on Shanice's face, forcing her to look away. After getting her emotions under control, she turned back to Queenie, her voice tight, eyes blazing anger. "That's what you want to do, for real? I don't have no say in this? You do what you want?"

"I gotta do what's best for me, baby. I got killas on my ass, and you or Pop Squad ain't enough. I need Pop. I got love for you, Shanice. You are an amazing woman, but I'm in way too deep. If you stay with me, you gon' inherit my beef, and I don't want that. Pop won't want it, either."

"Fuck Pop!" Shanice exploded. "Don't you see what he doin' to you? What he already did? He almost got you killed. You can't go back to him. It's gon' be the same thing all over again. Let him and D.D. kill each other. I don't care. Just don't go back."

"I'm sorry, baby, but I gotta do it. I tried to make it. I tried to put us on, but it didn't work, and now we in more shit. This the way it gotta be. Go back to yo' daughter and love on that li'l girl. I won't be able to forgive myself if somethin' happens to you. Get out while you can. I'm tellin' you this it because I love you. You gotta leave me. I'm marked for death."

Shanice remained stubborn. "No. I'm not leaving you. I'ma see this out."

***

"So, what we gon' do, Queenie? What's the next move?" Deso asked as he and Pop Squad lounged around the living room smoking blunts.

"I don't know, Deso." Queenie said, tapping blunt ashes into a green ceramic ashtray that sat on the table. "Skittlez had all the plugs. This was her neck of the woods. Without her, we movin' blind. I didn't make no plugs while I was here 'cause I was all in with Pop."

"What about Aloe?" La'Qua asked. "Last time we was out wit' them niggas, they was on our pussies. Him and his niggas got money. Me, you, and Shanice could probably set somethin up. One last move."

Deso, Drama, and Snot's eyes flicked to Queenie. Their eagerness to get on the grind shown on their faces.

"He was one of Skittlez's niggas, too," Queenie said. "Ain't no tellin' how fast news about us setting up Fly Boys got around. Them niggas might know about us already."

"That's why y'all gotta move fast," Drama spoke up. "Hit them niggas tonight. I think that shit wit' Fly Boys burnt us up and put us on the map. I think we should try to make this one last move before we blow this bitch."

"I'm wit' Drama," Snot said.

"We gotta leave anyway," La'Qua shrugged. "Might as well try to put some more money in the bag before we go."

Deso listened to the opinions of his team before turning to Queenie. "Since we fucked up the last move, I'ma let you call this. What you wanna do?"

Even though she had the final say, Queenie knew if she said no, the team would be mad. They wanted more money. They were hungry for it. They had already spent twenty of the sixty grand they took from ATM.

"I really don't like moving without planning first, but this is a desperate time. Me and the girls gon' find a way to get in contact wit' these niggas. Y'all wait on my call. Don't move 'til I say so."

"You got it, boss lady," Deso smiled, happy she agreed. "We move when you say so."

"And one more thing," Queenie said, getting everyone's attention. "I really don't know how to say this, so I'ma just say it. I don't know how much longer I'ma be wit' y'all. Once I find Pop and my sister, I'm leavin'."

Everyone was silent as the words registered in their minds.

"I knew you was on some ho-ass shit!" Drama mugged.

"Betta watch yo' mouf, nigga!"

"Or what, punk-ass bitch?" Drama said, getting up and walking toward the female boss.

The ashtray was in Queenie's hand so fast no one noticed her pick it up. Without missing a beat, she swung it at Drama's head like it was Thor's hammer. The ceramic shattered, cutting the side of his face, dropping him to the floor. "I told you to watch yo' mouf, nigga!"

"Bitch!" Snot screamed, charging Queenie.

Deso grabbed him around the waist, holding him back. "Nah, li'l brah. That nigga was talkin' shit and got fucked up. This ain't got nothin' to do witchu."

"Fuck that shit, Deso! She fuckin' wit' Pop Squad, she fuckin' wit' me!" Snot screamed, trying to wrestle free.

While Deso and Snot tussled, La'Qua went to check on Drama. He lay on the floor, blood leaking from the facial wound.

"She Pop Squad 'til she leave," Deso defended Queenie. "Chill out. You ain't finna touch her. Fall back."

After a little more wrestling, Snot calmed enough for Deso to let him go. Then the Pop Squad leader turned to Queenie. "What's this shit about you leavin'? I thought you was wit' us?"

"Trust me, Deso. It's best if I leave. Some shit followed me from Atlanta, and I don't want to get y'all in it. These niggas lookin' for me, Pop, and my sister. They already in Texas and killed my uncle. I gotta get back to Pop so we can take care of this."

Deso looked ready to kill. "What! Some niggas killed yo' uncle? When?"

"This mornin'. I made a deal wit' this nigga after he took me from the hospital to get them Pop so I could live. I ain't been able to find him, and these niggas think I'm playin'. Now they comin' for me."

"Whatever problems you got wit' them niggas is all our problems now. You Pop Squad, and we don't run from shit!"

***

Aloe had an unassuming look. Standing five-foot-seven with a light build, peanut butter-brown skin, and slanted eyes, the gold-rimmed glasses, polo shirt, white slacks, and loafers gave him a preppy look. However, the tattoos on his arms and neck gave away any misconceptions about him being a nerd. Despite the innocent look in his eyes, Aloe was certified in the streets. He embodied the TI lyrics 'articulate, but still a grab-a-nigga-by-the-collar quick.'

"I think Trump is a moron, racist, bitch-ass nigga, but he do got some gangsta-like qualities that you gotta respect. Yeah, I think he a ho-ass nigga that don't give a fuck about nobody but rich white niggas, but he ain't no bitch," Aloe explained to everyone seated around the living room in the trap house they affectionately called Central America. "Think about if Obama was on some shit like that. Said 'fuck all white people' and only fucked with black people. That nigga woulda only lasted one term in the Whitehouse, but he'da left a mark on the world, and real gangstas woulda respected that."

"Man, they woulda killed that nigga," Moose said, his name fitting him perfectly. Six-foot-four and 350 pounds with a head the size of a large pumpkin, the massive man commanded attention, even when he didn't want it.

"Hell, nah!" Aloe waved him off. "This America, nigga. Ain't nobody killin' no American President. The Secret Service ain't go in for that shit. If that's the case, Trump woulda got whacked day one wit' all the muthafuckas he pissed off. That nigga talked shit to North Korea, China, and Russia. He know he the baddest muthafucka walkin' and ain't worried 'bout shit."

"Is this what y'all do?" La'Qua interrupted. "Sit around and get fucked up and talk politics?"

Aloe looked offended by the question. "See, this the problem wit' black people. If niggas ain't talkin' 'bout killin' each other, bands to make her dance, or new cars, then they don't wanna hear shit. Never mind we lead the nation in poverty, incarceration, joblessness, high school drop-outs and infant mortality. All we wanna do is get high, drunk, and laugh about shit that ain't really funny."

La'Qua's face dropped at the eloquent tongue-lashing and sharp stare of the street veteran.

Shanice knew her girls were out of their leagues and spoke up to show they weren't fine and brainless. "I think it's refreshin' to hear niggas talk about somethin' other than killin' niggas and gettin' money. I haven't heard street niggas talk like this before, and I think it's sexy when a nigga can teach me somethin'. I hope whoever you got at home appreciate how rare of a nigga you is."

Aloe eyed the light-skinned beauty like he was seeing her for the first time. "Where you go to school at? College, I mean? I can tell you had a formal education by the way you put yo' words together."

"I graduated from The University of Texas with a bachelor's. I majored in economics."

Aloe gave a nod of approval. "I don't mean no disrespect by this, but I gotta ask. If you educated, why you kickin' it wit' strippers? Shouldn't you be usin' that degree?"

Shanice blushed from the attention. "I was. I mean, I am. I used to work at a bank, but I'm taking a leave to figure some things out. And these are my girls. I love them like family, and I'm down for them just like they down for me."

"I like you, shorty. You intriguing," Aloe smiled, eyeing her with desire. "Come sit next to me and let's kick it. I think I might've just found my wife."

While Aloe and Shanice got to know one another, Queenie set her eyes on a young, dark-skinned nigga named Hawke. Tall and lanky with a nappy afro and chinky eyes, he seemed like the perfect victim to set in a pussy trap. He hadn't talked much and seemed to be self-conscious and unsure. When Queenie gave him eye contact, he smiled and looked away.

"How old is you?" she asked.

The youngster couldn't hold his grin as he answered. "Eighteen."

"Yo' young ass is fine. Betcha you used to have all those li'l bitches at yo' high school goin' crazy."

The youngster smiled again, fidgeting nervously.

"You wastin' yo' time wi' that li'l nigga," Aloe laughed. "My li'l brotha can't handle somethin' like you."

Queenie went over and sat next to him, massaging his thigh as she spoke. "I don't care what yo' brother say. I like that you a li'l shy. You bein' you. Don't be like these other super-frontin'-ass niggas. My name is Queenie. You Hawke, right?"

"Yeah," he nodded, eyeing the cleavage that spilled from her halter-top.

"I like that name," Queenie laughed, watching his eyes. "You see somethin' you like?"

He gave a goofy grin. "You bad."

The seducer slid a hand further up his thigh. "Do you got a car? I'm kinda hungry."

Hawke looked toward Aloe for approval. The older brother nodded. "I got a G-Wagon. Wanna ride?"

"Yeah. Let's get outta here so I can put somethin' in my stomach."

During the ride to Popeye's, Hawke didn't do much talking, so Queenie exchanged text messages with Pop Squad, putting everything in order in case they got the opportunity to make a move. When they made it back to Central America, Shanice pulled Queenie aside and filled her in on everything that happened while she was gone.

"Aloe want me to spend the night with him."

Queenie's eyes popped. "At his house?"

"Yeah. You and Hawke, too."

Queenie's eyes lit up, a smile spreading across her face. "I didn't think it would be this easy."

"We got a gold mine between our legs, bitch. These niggas trynna get rich," Shanice laughed.

"You takin' to this jack shit too good," Queenie grinned. "I hope you don't get used to this."

***

During the ride to Aloe and Hawke's pad, the couples toyed and teased one another like they were high school sweethearts in the back of a limo on their way to prom. Once inside the house, more drinks were poured and loud smoked. Queenie made sure not to get too drunk, plotting a way to get Pop Squad in the house. It turned out the hustler's pad was protected by an alarm system, and security cameras watched every angle outside. There was no way for Pop Squad to get in without being seen.

"Okay. I had enough of the social hour," Queenie said, standing and reaching for Hawke's hand. "Come show me what they taught you in sex ed."

The youngster gave another goofy grin as he stood and led Queenie to his bedroom.

"Take it easy on my li'l nigga!" Aloe called behind them.

As soon as the room door closed, Queenie shoved Hawke on the bed and climbed on top. With her tongue down his throat, she felt up his bony body, making it seem like she was freaking him as she checked him for weapons. When she found the .45 at his waist, she dropped it on the floor, getting it as far from him as she could without seeming suspicious. "You a sexy li'l nigga," Queenie said, eyeing him like he was a snack. "Get up and take this shit off. I got somethin' special for yo' ass."

Hawke jumped up from the bed and stripped like he was in a contest to see who could get undressed the fastest.

When he was naked, Queenie pushed him onto the bed again. "Gimme somethin' to tie you up with?"

The shy kid frowned, suspicion lighting in his eyes. "Hell nah. You ain't finna tie me up."

Queenie was a little caught off guard by his response. Figuring she had the youngster figured out, getting a 'no' from him was concerning. But she played it off cool, kneeling between his legs and grabbing his hard tool. She held his stare while slipping the head into her mouth, going halfway down. After a few more head bobs, she swallowed him, her nose touching his pubic hair.

"Mm! Shit!" Hawke groaned, closing his eyes and reaching for her head.

Queenie dodged his hand, releasing his tool from her mouth. "You liked that, didn't you?"

"Hell, yeah!" he said, wanting more.

"Gimme a rope or a string and I'ma make yo' ass scream," she promised, slurping on him again.

Hawke lost all concern for his safety when she took away the warmth of her mouth. "I got some belts in the top drawer."

Queenie grabbed two Gucci belts, tying one around his ankles and another around his wrists. After checking to make sure they were secure, she stuffed a pair of boxers in his mouth and picked up the .45 from the floor.

"Damn, li'l nigga. I thought yo' ass had me figured out for a minute. But that head get 'em every time. Deep throat vicious, ain't it?" she smiled.

Hawke mugged her, the shy guy gone, replaced by an angry man who wanted vengeance. He mumbled something and tried to get up. A kick to the chest put him back on the bed.

"Keep yo' ass still 'fore I put a hole in yo' face," Queenie threatened, pointing the gun at him. "I need that alarm code."

He shook his head no.

Queenie moved the pistol to his nuts and began stabbing his balls with the barrel of the gun. The younger man squirmed and wiggled in pain.

"What's the code, nigga?" she whispered, threatening to poke him again.

He began mumbling.

"You gon' tell me the code?"

He nodded.

"Show me wit' yo' hands," she said, refusing to take the gag out of his mouth.

After he signed four numbers, Queenie grabbed her phone and called Deso. "What's good?" he answered eagerly.

"Where y'all at?"

"We outside. Y'all good in there?"

"Yeah. I got one nigga tied up. Shanice in the room wit' Aloe. I'm about to open the door. Come right in, and cover y'all face. He got cameras. I'ma flip the porch light off when I get the door open."

After hanging up, she gave Hawke one last look. He lay on the bed, seething with anger. When she was satisfied he wouldn't be trouble, she went to check on Shanice and Aloe. The living room was empty, a good sign they were in the room getting freaky. She didn't bother to get nosey, but went to deactivate the alarm.

After she put in the four numbers, there was a short beep, and then a message flashed across the screen saying the alarm had been turned off. She found the light switch and flipped it off before unlocking the door.

"Fuck you doin', bitch?"

Hearing Aloe's voice made her jump. Instead of turning around, she looked over her shoulder and seen the eloquent thug standing shirtless and holding a chopper. Because she had her back to him, he couldn't see the pistol in her hand, but she knew if she made the wrong move, he would cut her in half.

"I'm just trynna go outside real quick."

"You think I'm stupid? I got camera monitors in my room. Lock that door back and turn around slow. Where my li'l brother?"

Queenie knew she was fucked. If she locked the door and Pop Squad couldn't get in, she would die. If Aloe seen the gun, she would die. Her only hope was to get her niggas in the house, so she stalled. "C'mon, Aloe. Hawke in the room. I just wanna go—"

A loud noise near Hawke's room made Queenie look. So did

Aloe. Hawke's naked ass hopped into the hallway, his feet and hands still tied. In his hands an M-16.

Queenie processed the situation quickly, knowing she only had two options: try to run and probably get shot in the back, or use the distraction Hawke created and shoot it out. In the end, she knew she would lose the shooting match since she was up against two machine guns.

Her fate decided, she spun around, upping the pistol, planning to take one of the brothers with her. At the same moment the front door burst open, hitting Queenie, knocking her off balance. As she was falling to the floor, Hawke and Aloe were pointing their assault rifles at the door.

The high-powered rifles sounded like thunder as they erupted. Out of the corner of her eye, she could see Deso charging into the house. The bullets made smacking sounds as they ripped open the goon's chest and stomach.

Moving on instinct and adrenaline, Queenie pointed the .45 at the closest brother and let him have it. Hawke flinched a couple of times before falling to the floor.

Drama and Snot stood outside the front door, taking shots at Aloe. When he ducked out of the young gunners' sights, Queenie pointed the .45 at him, taking him down with two shots to the chest.

"Aw, shit!" Drama cried when he seen Deso lying on the ground in a pool of blood.

"Deso! Get up, nigga!" Snot yelled, his voice shaky, tears welling in his eyes.

Even though Queenie felt remorse for her fallen friend, she had to stay focused on the mission. "He dead. Come help me find the security videos."

Drama and Snot couldn't move. They stood over their fallen leader, mourning and confused.

Queenie ignored the broken thugs and went for Aloe's room. The wounded man was still alive, crawling to his chopper. A .45 slug to the back of the head ended any chance of his survival.

Inside the room, Shanice was sitting on the bed, fear swirling inside her wide eyes. "What happened?"

Queenie moved to the security monitors. "We gotta get the fuck outta here. Do you know how to find the footage?"

"Um. I don't know."

"Hold this." Queenie said, tossing her the .45 as she continued to look over the monitors. A few moments later she found the flash drive. "I got it. Let's go!"

Shanice gasped at the carnage when they left the room. Bullet holes in the wall and dead bodies on the floor made the living room look like a war zone.

"I got the footage. Let's go," Queenie told the Pop Squad members.

"Nah," Drama cried. "We can't leave him."

"He dead. We gotta go."

"Fuck that!" Snot snapped. "We ain't leavin' my nigga!"

While they went back and forth about Deso's body, no one noticed Hawke crawling slowly to his gun. Blood pooled from his stomach and chest wounds as he grabbed the gun and aimed it at Queenie's back. Shanice finally noticed the wounded youngster as he was applying pressure to the trigger.

Clap, clap, clap, clap!

Click.

Queenie flinched, spinning around to see what happened. Shanice's eyes were wide in shock. In her hand was the .45 with a de-cocked chamber.

"What the fuck?" Queenie asked.

Shanice looked from the dead body of Hawke to her girl. "He was about to shoot you."

Queenie looked back to Hawke. His dead body still held the gun. "Good shit. Let's go. Where's La'Qua?"

"She still in the car," Drama said sadly. "C'mon, Snot. Help me get Deso to the car."

"He dead, y'all. We gotta go, and a dead body gon' slow us down. C'mon."

Snot turned to Drama, agreeing with Queenie. "She right, dawg. We gotta get the fuck outta here and leave him."

J-Blunt

Chapter 14

The frankincense incense let off a thick trail of perfumed smoke as it burned, filling the room with a rich, sweet smell. Pop Somethin' inhaled deep as he lay on the massage table, his naked body mostly exposed except for the towel covering his ass. A female masseuse worked on his shoulders, digging into his flesh, kneading his muscles.

"Mm, shit. Damn," Pop grunted, loving the woman's touch.

"Damn, baby. You sound like you do when I be puttin' this pussy on you," Princess laughed, squeezing his hand. She was on the table next to him, getting a massage from an assistant.

"If I had to choose between you and her hands, you might be mad at me," he joked, making everyone laugh.

Princess sat up on her elbows, eyeing the woman bringing Pop so much pleasure. "Getcho hands off my man, Marjorie!"

The middle-aged Haitian woman put her hands in the air like she was being arrested and smiled. "I no want him, no. Too much man. Too big," she said in a heavy accent.

"You don't know what you missin'. Tell her, Ava. Bigger is better," Princess said to the assistant.

"When it big, it hit all the deep spots," she smiled.

After another round of laughter, Princess let out a long, satisfied sigh. "Damn, Pop. I feel better than I have in a long time. Jacksonville ain't bad. Why we didn't come here before we went to Atlanta?"

"We had to go through all the bullshit in Texas and the ATL so we would really be able to appreciate all the good shit in Florida. Super Trap exactly what we needed."

"He kinda remind me of C-Note. Except a li'l more gutta."

Pop thought for a moment. "Yeah, he do. And he smarter, too. That nigga turned The Zone into The Carter times ten."

Princess frowned. "What is The Carter?"

The big man gave Princess the side-eye. "You neva seen *New Jack City*?"

"Nah. What is it? Who in it?"

"Wesley Snipes played Nino Brown. Nigga was–. You know what? I'ma order it tonight. We watchin' it when we get to the crib. You gon' like the bitch they got on the team. She be blazin' shit. Her catchphrase is 'Rocka-bye, baby!'"

"So, we Netflixin' and chillin' tonight?"

"I don't know. I'ma hit The Zone and make sure they good. See if Super Trap need anything."

"A'ight. I was thinkin' 'bout what we gon' do after Florida. Still wanna go to Jamaica?"

"Hell yeah. Get away from all this drama shit. See the fam. It's been over twenty years since I been there. I don't know what up wit' moms. I ain't talked to her since I was little."

"Damn. I bet that'll be crazy, seein' her after so long. I wanna be there when you meet her."

"You will."

The couple became silent as they got massages and collected their thoughts. Marjorie broke the silence. "Would you like to listen to music?"

"What you got for a playlist?" Princess asked.

"I got love songs."

"I don't do love songs," Pop spoke up.

"Ain't nothin' wrong wit' love songs," Princess laughed, slapping him on the arm. "Go 'head. He will be okay."

When Ava turned on the radio, *Fall for You* by Leela James filled the room. Princess got lost in the lyrics, and when the song was over, she asked for it to be put on repeat.

"Damn, Pop. I love this song! This bitch is the truth!"

"It's a'ight," he mumbled.

"This song explains exactly how I feel, baby. I was trynna figure out a way to tell you this, and now I know. I'm in love with you, Pop. Being with you feels good. Like flying. Just like she singin'."

"You really wanna talk about this now?" Pop asked, looking at Ava uncomfortably.

"Why not? It's on my heart, and I need to get it off. I told you I didn't wanna be yo' bitch no more. When I said I wanted to be all yours and you all mine, this what I was talkin' 'bout. For the first time in my life, I'm in love. Now I know what they been singin' 'bout in all those love songs. I feel it."

"Want us to give you a moment?" Marjorie asked.

"Yes. Please."

When the women left the room, Princess got off her table and sat next to Pop. She stared into his eyes, searching the depths of him. "Do you love me? I mean, in love with me?"

For the first time in a long time, Pop didn't know how to answer a question. He cared for Princess. They were connected on a deep level. And just like she had felt the song lyrics, he did, too. But he'd never told anyone he loved them, and the thought of saying it made him unsure. "Listen, Princess. This love shit is new to me. I never been in love before, and I'm not sure how this shit s'posed to go. I don't know if I feel how you feel. All I know is this shit gettin' serious. Gettin' real."

Princess's eyes became misty. "I think this is what love is. We in love."

Pop didn't look convinced. "A'ight."

She reached out and touched his face, caressing his beard. "I love you, baby."

"A'ight."

Princess frowned. "That ain't what you s'posed to say to somebody you love. Say it back to me."

Pop visibly struggled to get the words out of his mouth. "I. I love you, too."

The mist in Princess' eyes turned to water as tears spilled down her face. "That wasn't so hard, now was it?"

"Actually, it was."

"Shut up!" she laughed, pushing him. "Now come kiss me, my love."

Pop kept his eyes open as he leaned in to lock lips. "Did I tell you how much I love the blue hair?" he asked, running a hand through her dreads.

"It ain't hard for you to say you love my hair, but it's hard to say you love me, huh?"

"Blue my favorite color," he smiled.

"I know. Now tell me you love me again," Princess said, melting her body into his.

Pop wrapped her blue dread locks around his fist and tugged. "I love yo' blue hair. And I love you, too."

The lovebirds began making out again, the petting getting hot and heavy as Pop pulled her onto his lap. Princess reached for his tool at the same time his phone rang. It was Super Trap's ringtone.

"Damn. What he want?" Princess asked, irritated by the interruption.

"I don't know, but let me get it real quick," he said before answering. "What up, my dude?"

"I need you to come through The Zone, brah. We got a situation that need yo' attention."

***

Ever since The Zone had come under new management, the residents noticed a decline in shootings and crime overall in the projects. There were no more shootouts and turf wars over who could move product where. It was understood that Out The Mud clique ran the projects, and Super Trap was the head nigga in charge. And although all the people living in the low income housing understood the power hierarchy, it appeared somebody didn't respect it.

Super Trap stood in the apartment they named Ground Zero looking at three bodies on the floor. The jackers were long gone with five kilos. "How the fuck they make it all the way to Ground Zero without nobody noticin'?" Trap asked, glaring angrily at Red Dot with his good eye.

"I don't know, brah. Didn't nobody see or hear shit. Only reason I came was 'cause Quan wasn't answerin' his phone."

Super Trap looked down at his dead friend's body again. Quan was face down on the ground, a bloody hole in the back of his head. Gold Cartier glasses rested in a pool of blood. "Did you talk to anybody? Where Dank and Paco?"

"Dank out there trynna see if anybody know anything. I ain't heard from Paco."

"Get somebody to clean this shit up. If you see Dank, tell him to get at me or Pop Somethin'," Trap said before heading for the door.

On his way out, he ran into Pop Somethin'. "What happened?" the big man asked.

"We got hit. Five birds. Quan, Triple T, and Rhino got hit. They in the living room."

Pop walked into the apartment and checked out the bodies. "Where Dank? Do anybody know anything?"

"Ain't nobody hear or see shit," Red Dot spoke, sniffing the air. "Why you smell like you been in one of them African stores?"

"I was gettin' a massage, and they had some incense burnin'. And what you mean, 'ain't nobody seen shit'? This Ground Zero. We in the middle of the projects. Ain't no way somebody made it in and outta here without bein' seen."

"I said the same shit," Super Trap spoke up. Then him and Pop looked to each other at the same time. "Inside job!"

"Ain't nobody stupid enough to fuck you niggas over," Red Dot said, convinced they were mistaken.

Super Trap gave his cousin a look. "You be surprised how stupid niggas is."

Pop's phone rang. It was Dank. "Where you at?"

"Down here by Veronica spot. Where you at?"

"I'm leavin' Ground Zero. Who is Veronica?"

"Li'l chick a few buildings away. I'm steppin' outside right now. You ain't gon' believe what she just told me."

When Super Trap and Pop Somethin' met up with Dank, the shorter man wore a smile like he knew something they didn't.

"What you smilin' for, nigga?" Trap asked.

"It was a set up," Dank grinned.

"We know," Pop said. "What else you know? Who did it?"

Dank frowned. "How y'all know that already? I had to talk to ten people to find that out."

"Deductive reasoning," Trap said. "Tell us what you know."

"The bitch said she seen Twan come through here wit' two niggas she never seen before. Said he looked nervous. She tried to holla at the nigga, but he kept movin'. Twan set us up."

"What we know 'bout this nigga, Twan?" Pop asked.

"Not that much. He was one of the niggas we made get down or lay down. This his backyard. I think he a local nigga," Dank answered.

"Find us somebody that know him. We gon' get down on his ass as soon as we can."

***

Theresa used to be a dime back in her heyday with soft skin the color of beach sand, silky jet-black hair that flowed to the middle of her back, and the petite frame of an Olympic gymnast. And then crack got ahold of her, turning the certified dime into a petty penny in a matter of months. Now Theresa hung out with the bottom feeders, spending every waking moment plotting ways to make money so she could get high.

She was currently in her son's room, trying to be as neat as she could, searching for money to cash in or drugs to ride that atomic blast to the moon. A loud knock on the front door interrupted her treasure hunt. After a quick look around to make sure everything was the way her son left it, she went to answer the door.

"Who is it?"

"Marty. Open up."

Dollar signs and a vision of a crack pipe between her lips flashed in her head as Theresa clicked the locks. Marty wasn't much to look at. Standing five feet, four inches and slightly overweight with thinning black hair, he did a bad job combing over the bald spot at the top of his head. But the white man was the answer to every crackhead's prayer: a pussy trick whose options were limited because of his lack of style and flavor. He was a regular at Theresa's house on payday.

"Hey, baby!" Theresa smiled, reaching out to embrace her Friday night event.

Marty received the embrace and held out the plastic flowers and bottle of cheap wine. "These are for you, babe. Let me in."

"Thank you so much," she said, taking the flowers and throwing them on the couch as he walked by. "I was wondering when I was gon' see you again. I missed you so much."

"You got anything? I'm ready to let loose."

"Nah, but come to my room and gimme yo' phone so I can call my son."

When they got to the room, Marty sat his cash on the table and stripped quickly. Theresa grabbed the phone and called her son.

"What up, Ma?"

"Bring me some work, boy. And hurry up."

"I told you, I ain't got shit right now."

"Nigga, quit lyin'. I got Marty over here, and we ready to turn up. Bring me a ball."

The youngster's tone change when she mentioned Marty. "I'm on my way."

After hanging up, Theresa turned to the chubby white man, rubbing his legs as she crawled his body. His little pink pecker began to grow the closer she got to it. "You look happy to see me. You want me to take care of this, don't you?"

Marty nodded his head up and down quickly, expectation in his eyes. "Yeah, baby. Take care of me and I'll take care of you."

Theresa wrapped three fingers around his meat and swallowed him whole. The square was no match for the Dominican street stalker. She sucked and licked him to a quick nut.

While she was swallowing his seed, there was a knock on the door. Anticipation of roasting a rock flashed in her mind as she sat the penis aside and grabbed the money from the table. "Be right back, baby," she called to Marty, leaving the room. "Why don't you got yo' key, boy?" Theresa questioned as she got to the front door, unlocking it.

Instead of seeing her son standing on the stoop, Theresa stared into the eyes of Dank. Next to him was Pop Somethin'. "Who is y'all? What y'all want?" she asked, copping an attitude.

"Twan here?" Dank asked.

"Nah. Who is y'all?" she asked, eyeing them suspiciously.

"I'm Dom. Do you know where he is?"

"Nah, I don't know where he at. He don't live here."

Realizing they would get nowhere being civil, Pop turned hostile, shoving the little woman into the house and forcing his way in.

"Hey! Get out my house! Getcho hands off me!"

"Shut the fuck up, bitch!" Pop growled, pulling a Desert Eagle. "Where the fuck is Twan? This yo' last chance."

"H-he not here right now," she stuttered, eyeing the gun like it was a deadly snake. "What the fuck he do now?"

"He crossed the wrong nigga," Dank said, locking the door. "Where the fuck yo' son at, and how can we find him?"

"I just told you, he don't–"

"What's going on out here?" Marty asked, standing in the bedroom doorway wearing a pair of boxers. When he seen Pop Somethin' and Dank, he tried to creep back into the room.

"Getcho ass back out here!" Pop yelled, charging the room and catching Marty trying to make a call. "Dial a number and I'ma blaze yo' bitch-ass!"

Marty dropped the phone and put his hands up. "Please, man! I don't want any trouble! I just came over to get laid and have a good time."

"You know who Twan is?"

Marty's eyes brightened. "Yeah. That's her son. He's on his way over right now. I can give you his number if you want. Just let me leave."

Pop took some of the aggression out of his voice. "You did everything I needed you to do. Good lookin'. You can leave."

Relief washed over the white man's face as he reached for his clothes. "Thanks so much, man. I don't even really know Theresa or her son. I just came over to get a blow job and get high. I never even seen you, man."

"Your word is your bond," Pop grinned.

"That's right, brother," Marty nodded, sliding into his pants. "Word is bond."

Pop laughed again before lifting the gun and shooting Marty in the face.

When he walked back into the living room, Theresa was pleading with Dank.

"Please, don't kill me, young man. I don't know what my son did, but I'm sorry. He don't live here, and I ain't seen him in a couple days. Whatever problems y'all got wit' him–"

"Twan on his way right now," Pop cut her off. "That's what the white boy said."

Theresa's eyes grew wide as full moons. "Uh. I-I didn't mean to. Uh. I'm sorry. Please don't kill me."

"You good," Pop told her. "Have a seat. We gon' figure this out when yo' son get here."

"Do you mind if I go grab a cigarette? Y'all havin' these guns got a bitch scared. My nerves goin' crazy."

"Tell me where they at. I'll get 'em."

"In my bedroom. Should be on the dresser."

Pop went to grab the cigarettes and a lighter. Theresa sat on the couch and chain smoked while rocking back and forth, mumbling about her son's bullshit. Ten minutes later, a key was inserted into the lock on the front door.

When Twan walked into the house, he immediately noticed Pop Somethin' standing next to his mother. The seriousness of the situation only took a moment to register in his mind. His eyes grew wide and he spun to run back out of the house.

Dank anticipated the move and swung the .357 Magnum at his head like it was a Louisville Slugger. "Lay yo' bitch-ass down!" Dank yelled.

"You was gon' leave yo' momma in here wit' some goons?" Pop asked, shaking his head at the chump balled up on the floor.

"C'mon, Pop! I didn't do nothin'," Twan whined.

"So, whatchu runnin' for?"

"'Cause y'all in my house. I know y'all ain't come here to kick it."

"You right. I came for my dope. Where my shit at, nigga?"

"I don't know what you talkin' 'bout. I'm Out the Mud. We eat together."

Pop put the .50 caliber in his mother's face. "Lie to me again, nigga, and I'ma push yo' momma shit back."

"Quit lyin', boy! Tell him where his shit at!" Theresa yelled.

"Okay, mane! Okay!" Twan cried. "I left it wit' Radical."

"Who the fuck is Radical?" Dank asked.

"My baby momma brother. He Goon Squad."

Pop looked disgusted by the sight of the traitor. "This what I get for puttin' you on, huh? Bit the hand that feed you?"

"C'mon, Pop. I'm sorry, brah. I didn't mean–"

Pow!

Theresa's head jerked violently as the Desert Eagle slug exploded out the back of her head.

"Momma!" Twan cried.

A .357 bullet from Dank's Magnum stopped the scream, ending the back-stabber's life.

Chapter 15

J-West was a hard man to please. He wore the 'seen it all, done it all' attitude on his chest like it was the charm on a necklace. Standing a few inches over six feet tall with a frame as wide as a doorway, the 290-pound man looked as intimidating as a Blue Ribbon Bull.

"Nigga, these bitches betta be er'thang you say they is. My bitch Tuti can suck the chrome off Forgies, and I'm missin' out on that right now," J-West barked, spilling Patron on the table as he poured another shot.

"My nigga, they fucked a double-sided dildo at the last party," Radical said, the impression left by the women showing in his eyes. "This dark-skinned bitch with blue dreads so muthafuckin' sexy. Wait 'til you see these hos get down."

"That shit live, brah," Derion added. "My li'l duck-off bitch, Star, bad wit' a bad attitude."

"So, who fuckin' the bitch wit' the blue dreads?" J-West asked.

"That's me," Radical smiled proudly.

"That ain't chu, nigga. Quit lyin' on yo' dick," Derion laughed.

"I ain't say I fucked, nigga. I said that's me."

"Since she ain't cho bitch, I got dibs, nigga," Laro spoke up, waving his case in the air. He had been out of the hospital for a few weeks and was back with the team fulltime. Standing only five-foot-seven and 160 pounds, the twenty-two-year-old was looked at as a little brother by most of Goon Squad.

"Bitch too much for yo' delicate ass!" J-West laughed. "Yo' bones ain't even finished healin' yet. You can't handle these professional hos right now. You gotta go get some school bitches first. Start off wit' some good girls."

Laro dropped the ash off his blunt and smiled. "I love good girls, nigga. They the baddest ones."

The ringing of Derion's phone made everyone pause. "Look at chu niggas," he laughed, reading the text. "Hos 'bout to come through, and y'all don't know how to act."

J-West picked up a couch pillow and threw it at him. "Just let 'em in, fool-ass nigga!"

From the porch, Derion watched the women exit the green, rented Buick Envoy. Princess led the way wearing a white mini dress that formed to the curves of her hips, making it look like she was rocking a glass of milk. Her blue dreadlocks bounced around every time she took a step on the pavement.

Tanya followed walking the sidewalk like it was a catwalk. Pink Fendi heels showed manicured toes, the matching pink dress flexed a body made to lust after as the woman with new money strutted confidently, knowing she attracted attention whenever she walked in a room.

Star brought up the rear, putting an extra switch in her hips, loving the way their presence mesmerized Derion. She wore black leggings, a red half-shirt with 'Bossy' written across the front, and black-and-red retro Jordans. She also carried an overnight bag full of goodies

"Y'all came out that bitch like Destiny Child!" Derion grinned, openly lusting after the women as they walked up onto the porch. He gave Star a lingering stare. "I know you leavin' wit' me after we done. Came through this muthafucka lookin' like somethin' sweet to eat!"

"Boy, you crazy!" the thotty stripper laughed, giving him a delicate embrace.

When the women walked in the house, Goon Squad eyed them like they were prey.

"What's poppin', ladies?" J-West spoke. "Y'all come in. Maintain wit' Goon Squad for a li'l while. My niggas been sayin' good shit 'bout ch'all. I'm J-West. Tell me y'all names."

The women took turns introducing themselves.

"Okay. Y'all rest off ya feet for a li'l while. Smoke wit' us and pop a bottle. Start the show when y'all ready. Don't keep me waitin' too long, though. I know y'all er'thang my niggas said y'all was."

Blunts got puffed and liquor was drank as the ladies and gangstas got better acquainted. When they were ready, Star pulled a collapsible pole from her overnight bag and began setting it up while Princess handled the music.

When Rihanna's *Sex with Me* filled the room, Tanya stalked toward the stripper pole like a model. She twisted and turned on the metal rod, expressing sexy in every facial expression and pose as she turned the men on, dancing like she had been in the club for years. The dress came off a few minutes later and she did the splits, twerking her backside to the rhythm of the Rihanna track.

Princess and Star watched from the sidelines as their caterpillar bloomed into a butterfly right before their eyes.

When the song was over, Tanya began to work the crowd, giving lap dances while Princess took to the pole. The blue-haired vixen slithered around it like a sexy snake, wrapping her body around the pole, up and down, all around the floor, and then back up the pole again. When the mini-dress came off, she dropped to her knees, jiggling her ass and clapping her cheeks. Goon Squad cheered as the blue-haired woman danced like she was made to turn niggas on.

When the song changed, she dug into the trick bag and pulled out two chain leashes attached to collars. One went around Tanya's neck, the other around Star's. Princess had the women get on their hands and knees, leading them around the room like they dogs. After giving the men and a good view of their lady parts, Star positioned herself behind Tanya and began sniffing her ass. Loving the feel of her friend's nose between her cheeks, Tanya put her face on the floor and hiked her ass high into the air. Star began licking her thong-covered pussy through the fabric, making Tanya moan in pleasure.

"Take them muthafuckas off!" J-West cheered.

"Eat that shit from the back!" Laro added.

Star gave the crowd what they wanted when she pulled down Tanya's thong and began eating her from the back.

Princess allowed the women a few moments of pleasure before yanking Star's leash, pulling her away from Tanya. "Get a toy out the bag, Star. Tanya, lay across J-West's knees."

Tanya crawled onto J-West's knee, positioning her ass in the air like she was about to get a spanking. J-West's 'seen it all, done it all' ego was set aside as the brown-skinned beauty with a fat ass lay on his leg when he caressed and I admired her backside.

"You like that?" Princess asked the big man, noticing the look of desire on his face.

"You know I do," J-West grinned.

"Well, spank her ass, then. She love that shit."

After giving her ass a few more rubs, he slapped her cheeks lightly. Tanya moaned, hiking her ass higher into the air. "That ain't shit, nigga. Hit it harder," Tanya demanded.

He did as requested, spanking her ass, loving the way her soft flesh jiggled under his hand.

"You wanna fuck her?" Star asked, holding out a thick, black, eight-inch dildo.

The goon snatched the sex toy. "You know I do. Gimme that shit."

After applying lube to the dildo, Star spread Tanya's cheeks apart while J-West slipped the fake phallus inside. Derion, Laro, and Radical all craned their necks to get a better view.

"Oh, yeah!" Tanya moaned, digging her nails into his thighs.

The wetter her pussy got, the deeper J-West pushed the dildo. A few minutes later he was shoving the entire eight inches inside her and Tanya was pushing her ass back into his had, covering him with pussy juice.

"Do it faster! Gimme some more!" Tanya moaned.

J-West sped up, but it wasn't enough for the vixen. She was insatiable.

"Let me show you how to fuck a bitch," Star said, taking the dildo. She spread Tanya's ass apart with one hand and began licking her ass while ramming the dildo in and out of her as fast as her arm could move.

"Oh, yeah, bitch! Damn, that shit feel so good!" Tanya moaned as pleasure gripped her body.

Princess and the Goon Squad watched, transfixed by the sex scene unfolding before them. Tanya's sex faces, moans, and body movements had all the men adjusting themselves as bulges in their pants grew. And when Princess couldn't take the lust burning inside her anymore, she stepped out of her thong and walked over to Tanya. Being cousins didn't cross either of their minds as Princess grabbed ahold of Tanya's hair and pulled her face to her pussy.

J-West looked on in amazement as Tanya sucked Princess' pussy while Star licked her ass and fucked her with the dildo. He could feel pussy juice soaking the thigh of his jeans as the threesome unfolded on his lap. Goon Squad was so caught up in the show that nothing mattered but the climax.

A few moments later, cries of ecstasy filled the room as the women came. Goon Squad got an extra bang for their buck when Star stripped from her panties and another round of the threesome kicked off again.

When the women were satisfied and the men felt like they had gotten their money's worth, a lounge session happened and they kicked it. Radical sat next to Princess, Derion next to Star, and J-West had an arm wrapped around Tanya's shoulder.

"I seen you somewhere before, but I just can't remember," Laro said, eyeing Princess.

"Nah, I don't think so, baby. I just came from Georgia and only been here a couple months."

"I don't forget a face," Laro continued. "I seen you somewhere. It's gon' come to me eventually. But in the meantime, y'all the truth wit' the show y'all put on."

"Quit sweatin' her like that, nigga," J-West said, trying to impress Tanya. "They outta-towners. We gon' show them how Goon Squad do in Jacksonville. We all about havin' a good time."

"You see how we do. We all about fun," Tanya laughed, patting his hand that rested on her thigh.

"Well, how 'bout you come wit' me and we can have some fun?"

Tanya gave a coy grin. "I think you a boss and all that, and I respect you, J-West. I know what niggas say about you. The streets always talkin' 'bout you and yo' niggas. But I ain't no ho. What me and my girls did was part of the show. We 'bout getting' our coins. But I just don't be goin' home wit' niggas I don't know. Plus, I got a nigga."

J-West got cocky. "Yeah, yeah, I hear all that. But I want you, baby. And I always get what I want. You can keep that nigga. I got bitches, but I still wanna fuck witchu, and we need to make that happen."

"You know I can't say no to a nigga like you." Tanya smiled, rubbing his chest. "It's somethin' 'bout you I can't let go. I knew I would fuck witchu as soon as I walked in here. But I'm serious 'bout not givin' you no pussy right away. Not yet."

On the other side of the room, Radical seemed to be fairing better than his leader. "I ain't playin' no games, baby. I just hit a lick, and I'm trynna take you wit' me to Miami. Blow a bag. You comin' or what?"

Princess gave him a suspicious stare. "Don't be playin' wit' me, man. You can't play wit' a bitch 'bout shoppin' trips."

"What I just say?" Radical asked, staring at her seriously. "Me and my niggas just hit some niggas in The Zone for some birdies. I'ma make a couple moves, and then me and you gon' move out. No lie, baby. I told you I wanna make some move witchu. You down wit' a nigga or what?"

Princess gave his question some thought. "Damn, nigga. You trynna get me in trouble wit' my man."

"Fuck that nigga. Come on and go wit' me. I gotchu."

Princess paused to think again. "Okay. Fuck it. I'ma fuck witchu, Radical. But you bet not be playin' wit' me, nigga. I'm for real."

Radical smiled like the Grinch that stole Christmas, thinking he took Princess from her man. "You good, ma. For now, how 'bout we get outta here and go to my spot? I got a surprise for you."

***

Princess was surprised at how nice Radical's house was. A neatly-cut lawn and trimmed hedges made up the landscape. The brown and beige paint looked fresh, and on the inside, hardwood floors shined like they had been freshly waxed. A big screen TV, video game setup, and leather furniture made up the living room.

"Damn, Radical. You livin' good, baby," Princess said, impressed by his digs.

"Don't too many people get to come up in here. I gotta really fuck witchu to bring you to my shit."

"Well, I feel lucky," Princess smiled. "Can I use yo' bathroom? I wanna freshen up a li'l bit before you show me my surprise."

"Fo' sho. Bathroom down the hall. First door on the right. It's some towels in there, and some soap. I'ma have yo' surprise waitin' when you come out."

Princess decided to take Radical up on his offer to shower, but before she got in the water, she sent out a text.

After taking a quick shower, she wrapped a towel around her body and another around her dreads, then went to find Radical. He was sitting on the couch in the living room, wearing a smile big as a half moon. On the table in front of him was five kilos.

"Damn, baby. Is those what I think they is?" Princess smiled.

"Sparrows. Eagles. Birdies. I told you I made a move. Sometimes I gotta cut my niggas out and make my own moves. That's how I live the way I do. Some niggas live in the slums, but I ain't wit' that shit. I'm trynna leave this jack shit one day, and this might be my shot."

Princess sat next to him on the couch and began feeling up his body. "Damn, baby. I love the surprise. My nigga ain't neva did no shit like this. All that dope makin' my pussy wet."

Radical smiled, happy at the results the dope brought. He had been waiting to fuck Princess for a long time and was finally about to get his wish.

When he reached for the towel, Princess flung it open and spread her legs. "You seen what I like. Can you make me cum, nigga?"

Radical's smile grew wide as he pulled the pistol from his waist and sat it on the couch next to Princess before getting on his knees. He wasted no time snacking on her clit and sticking two fingers inside her womb.

Princess closed her eyes and gripped the couch pillows, enjoying the tongue-lashing. When her hand bumped into the steel of the pistol, a jolt of electricity shot through her body. The feel of the murder weapon had done something. She remembered what Queenie told her after she killed Nitty while she rode him. Said it was the best orgasm she ever had. Then there was the sexcapade in the shower after they killed the detective in Atlanta. That was the best orgasm Princess had ever had.

Thinking about the sexual situations with Queenie made her want to be closer to her sister. To feel what she felt. So she reached for the pistol, making sure the safety was off. The feel of the steel in her hand and thoughts of murder sent a shiver through her body as the orgasm came in a rush.

Pow!

Blood, brains, and skull squirted onto Princess as the orgasm took its time passing through her. It seemed like everything inside her had been put into a blender and pulverized, and was now seeping from her pussy. It took more than a minute for the climax to fade.

When she opened her eyes, Radical's face was still between her legs, blood leaking out the side of his head. As she stared at the dead man, she didn't feel any sorrow or remorse. In fact, the more she stared at the dead man and his blood covering her inner thighs, she liked it.

Then she began laughing. "Oh, my God! I am tripping."

After going to take another shower, she called Pop.

"I'm a few minutes away," he answered.

"I took care of everything. I got the packages, too."

Pop sounded surprised. "For real? Where he at?"

"On the floor. I'ma light this bitch up and take one of his cars. I don't think J-West knew about him taking from us. That was his side move. But they gon' know I did this."

"You know we don't fear none. And now we got a team and war-ready. Meet me in The Zone, and we gon' plot our next move."

Chapter 16

Super Trap stared at the seventy-inch HD screen a Wesley Snipes played Nino Brown in the hood classic *New Jack City*. In a lot of ways he could relate to the fictional drug dealer. In a matter of months he had gone from living in the projects and working as a janitor to being the face of a drug-dealing. organization that had taken over a local project. Money wasn't a problem anymore. He didn't have to worry about his daughter growing up in a roach-infested house or going to shitty public schools. Now he lived in a suburban mansion where crime, drugs, and rodents were a thing of the past. And when Yanna was old enough, she would go to the finest schools and rub shoulders with the children of politicians, moguls, and rich folk. And his woman was well taken care of, too. No more stripping and strangers groping her flesh for a couple hundred dollars. No more struggling to pay bills. Now she could lay back and reap the benefits of fucking with a boss nigga. Manis, pedis, shopping sprees, driving foreign cars. Super Trap was back.

Yet, despite the success, the money-man's mind was troubled. A storm was brewing, and the damage could tear the city apart.

"Where yo' mind at? Why you not watchin' the movie?" Tanya asked, rubbing the scar on Trap's face.

"A storm comin', baby, and I can't help but think about er'body that's gon' get caught up in it. I told you this money gon' bring us problems."

"Shit, bein' broke brought us problems, too. I'd rather have rich problems than broke ones."

"You say that because you haven't taken the L's I have. Baby, these streets is vicious. They will take everything. Niggas is heartless."

"So, y'all was just s'posed to let Goon Squad take y'all shit and not do nothin'?"

"Nah, I ain't sayin that. But a war comin' behind Radical gettin' knocked off. And J-West seen you, Star, and Princess faces. I'm worried about that."

"But we know more about them than they know about us. We

can hit them anytime. Plus, we got a project full of niggas ready to move when you or Pop Somethin' say so. I know I'm new to this, but I believe in you and that big-ass, crazy nigga. Y'all two comin' together was like Kevin Durant going to the Warriors. Unstoppable."

Trap cut his good eye at his girl. "Did you really just do that?" he laughed.

"What? I know about sports, nigga. Plus, it fits."

Trap smiled at Tanya. "Damn, I love yo' ass, girl. Every day you show me a new side of you."

"You wanna see somethin' else?" she asked, a lustful gleam in her eye. "I can do somethin' to help take yo' mind off the problems in the streets."

"You know I love fuckin' you, girl, but I need to think this out. I can't take J-West lightly. Goon Squad be wreckin' shit all over."

"What did Pop Somethin' say?"

"Him and Dank puttin' together a hit squad. When he get everything situated, I'ma go holla at 'em and see what they wanna do. But I ain't gon' leave it all in Pop lap because my face is on Out the Mud."

"Well, don't spend all night stressin' 'cause I want some dick before I go to sleep," Tanya said, reaching for her phone and going on Facebook.

Trap turned his attention back to the TV and thoughts back to J-West. They had to hit him hard and fast. If possible, start at the top and knock off the leader first, and the little guys would probably fall. But finding J-West wasn't easy. Yeah, they found out where Goon Squad gathered, but not where J-West lay his head. He wasn't sure if he should hit the gathering house and hope to catch J-West or wait it out.

"Oh, my God!" Tanya cried, looking at her phone like it had grown body parts.

"What happened?" Trap asked.

"Our uncle dead! I gotta call Princess and tell her."

***

Pop cut the engine of the black-on-black Jeep Liberty Sport, looking around for anything suspicious as he climbed out of the truck. When he was satisfied no one would jump out, he climbed the porch of his new three bedroom brick house. When he unlocked the door, a flowery smell tickled his nose and candles let off a soft glow all around the living room. Princess lay on the white leather couch dressed in black lingerie, sipping a glass of wine.

"Hey, baby," she smiled, grabbing a blunt off the table and greeting him at the door. "How was your day?"

Pop grabbed the weed, allowing Princess to light it. "I was a li'l stressed, but now that I'm home, I feel better. What up wit' the candles?"

"Come sit down and let me tell you," Princess said, leading him to the couch.

After Pop was seated, she handed him a flute of champagne and knelt between his legs to take off his shoes. *Cater To You* by Destiny's Child was playing in the background. "I was listening to this song earlier, and it made me want to show you how much I appreciate you. Tonight is about you, baby. I'm catering to you. Let me help you out these clothes."

Pop loved the special attention from his lady as she helped him strip down to his boxers and began massaging his feet.

"Pop, ever since I met you, you changed my life. You took me from runnin' the streets wit' a bunch of niggas that might get me killed to trips to Mexico on yachts and different states gettin' real money. I know what livin' the good life is because of you. Because of you, I know what trust is. What loyalty is. And I finally found out what love is. You got my heart, Pop. And I want you to have it forever. I don't know if you will ever believe in love the way I do, but I don't ever wanna be in love wit' nobody else but you."

Princess let go of his foot and reached under the couch, bringing out a gift-wrapped box. Inside were two rings. She took out a diamond-encrusted pinky ring and took ahold of his hand.

"I know you don't wanna get married the traditional way, so I'ma do the gangsta way. With this pinky ring, I give you my heart, my loyalty, and all my trust. You complete me. In you I found everything I ever wanted in a nigga. So, will you accept this ring and be my nigga? Nothin' won't separate us. This ain't no 'til death do us part. We ain't gon' neva end. Even when we gone."

Pop was lost for words. The proposal was unexpected, and he didn't know how to respond. Yeah, he told Princess he loved her and felt connected to her in a way he couldn't explain, but he would always remember what love had done to his uncle, Shanice's father. It made him a fool and got him killed.

As Pop stared into Princess' clear brown eyes, a question popped into his mind. *Would I die for her?*

He remembered hearing a verse from the Bible about no greater sacrifice than to lay down your life for someone you loved. He knew with absolute certainty Princess would die for him. The look of love reflecting on her face told how she worshipped him. He had become her everything. Her friend. Her lover. Her lord. He wasn't sure if he truly loved her the way she loved him, but not accepting the ring would crush her world. And he cared about her way too much to cause her pain.

"I wasn't expectin' this, baby, and you caught a nigga off guard. But what we got is forever. I accept yo' ring and yo' heart, and everything that come with it. I love you, girl."

Princess smiled like a super fan meeting Drake backstage as she slid the ring onto Pop's pinky.

He flexed his fist, admiring the new ice. "Now, that's gangsta."

"I got a ring, too, but we gon' worry 'bout that later," Princess said, slipping a diamond engagement ring onto her left ring finger. "I got one more surprise for you. Star!"

Pop turned at the sound of movement coming from the bedroom. Star sashayed into the living room wearing a red silk robe and a bra and thong set a size too small, making her curves appear more dangerous. She stopped in front of Pop and took off the robe, doing a turn to give him a look at all her assets. Thick thighs, a fat ass, and huge breasts had Pop ready to go.

"That was the most romantic gangsta shit I ever seen," she grinned.

Princess stood next to Star. "This our lifetime commitment gift, and I wanna share her with you, baby."

Pop's dick grew through the hole in his boxers as he watched the women make out. When Star seen it, her eyes popped. "Ooh! I knew you had a big dick," she said and knelt between his legs.

She wasted no time attacking his meat. When it came to giving head, Star was on top of her game. She used her hand, mouth, and lots of spit. Pop grunted, sucking in deep breaths of air.

Not wanting to feel left out, Princess knelt next to Star and began sucking his balls.

"Mm, shit!" Pop groaned as the women attacked his piece.

Then the women began passing him back and forth, each taking turns sucking on him. When he couldn't take any more, he busted. The ladies shared his cum in a wet and nasty tongue kiss.

Wanting more, Star sucked him into her mouth again, making sure he stayed hard. Then she climbed on top of him, reverse cowgirl, and slid down his pole.

Princess watched her friend ride her nigga, loving the noises and sex faces her and Pop made. "Take that dick, girl!" Princess cheered. When she had enough watching, she leaned forward and began sucking Star's clit while she rode Pop.

"Oh yeah, bitch!" Star moaned, grabbing Princess by the dreads and holding her face in place.

They continued until Star came, then changed positions. Princess climbed onto Pop's lap, impaling herself on his sword. Star stood over Pop, one foot on the couch and the other on the headrest as she put her pussy on his face. The big man licked and sucked her pussy while Princess bounced on his dick. Sounds of pleasure I filled the living room as the ménage heated up. They fucked all over the couch, floor, and living room, changing multiple positions until everyone got theirs. For the final scene, Star lay on the floor with her legs open, Princess stacked on top of her with her legs open, too. Pop crawled between their legs and took turns sticking dick to both of them. When he finally busted again, he collapsed on top of Princess, spent.

"Damn! Y'all some freaks, for real," Star breathed. "Let me up.

I need a drink of water after that shit. I think I'm dehydrated."

Pop rolled onto the floor, reaching for another blunt on the table. "I like her."

"Me, too. You wanna keep her?" Princess asked.

"Let's keep her around and see how it go."

When Princess' phone began vibrating, she picked it up and found a text from Tanya.

"Who dat?" Pop asked.

"Tanya sent me a text. She said to call her."

"See what she want."

Princess was already dialing the number. "Hey, girl. What's so important that you textin' me during my sex hours?"

"Damn, Princess," Tanya hesitated. "I don't know how to tell you this, but Uncle Larry dead."

It took a moment for the news to register in Princess' mind. "What you mean, he dead? How you know?"

"I just seen it on Facebook. Go on my page and look. His funeral is this weekend."

"What happened?" Princess asked. "How he die?"

"It say somebody killed him, but they don't know who," Tanya answered. "Just look at the comments online."

After hanging up, Princess went on Facebook to see what Tanya was talking about. It turned out to be true. Larry was dead. When the news finally hit home, tears began dripping down Princess' face. "Damn, baby. Somebody killed my uncle. I gotta go back to Texas. I need to be at the funeral. I need to know what happened."

Pop hated the thought of stepping foot in Texas. Gonzo had a green light on him, but he couldn't let Princess go alone, so he pulled her close, wrapping her in his arms. "We gon' go. Don't trip. We gon' figure out what happened to yo' uncle."

Star walked into the living room drinking a glass of ice water, looking refreshed. "A'ight. I'm ready. Let's get–" She paused when she seen the tears on Princess' face. "What happened? Did somebody die?"

Chapter 17

Being back in Texas felt surreal to Pop Somethin', like a déjà vu experience or out-of-body trip. And as he walked up on the porch of Princess' aunty's house, he couldn't help feeling coming back home was a mistake. The hair on the back of his neck stood up and goosebumps raced up and down his forearms. Something was wrong. He wasn't sure what it was, but his instincts never lied. Coming back to Texas was a mistake.

"I ain't feelin' this," Pop mumbled as Princess rang the doorbell.

"I know," she agreed. "It feel weird, don't it?"

Pop eyed his girl. "You feel it, too?"

"Hell yeah! I feel like the police or some nigga gon' jump out on our ass when we least expect it."

"My instincts ain't neva lied to me, baby. We gotta make this trip short as we can. After we leave here, we goin' to see Aunty Ruby so I can check on Deso, and then back to the telly."

"Who is it?" a woman called from behind the door.

"Princess."

When the door swung open, a dark-skinned woman with green highlights in her hair greeted Princess with a big smile. "Hey, cousin! Gimme some love, gurl!"

The women exchanged a long hug before Princess introduced her man. "Keysha, this my nigga, Pop. Pop, this my cousin."

"'Sup," he nodded.

"Hey, Pop. Y'all come in and sit down," Keysha offered. "Fucked up the only time we get together is after somebody die."

"It is, ain't it?" Princess agreed. "First my momma and now Larry. Do anybody know what happened?"

"Nah. It don't make sense. He didn't have no enemies. He was a workin' nigga. Worked at that damn factory since we was little. They found his body floatin' in the river, but the police said he got killed at home. Why would somebody go through all that trouble to take his body to the river? That don't make sense."

"What about his phone? Did they release his property to

anybody?"

"Momma got it. She the one that checked up on him. His phone was still at the house."

"Call her and get the last number he called and that called him," Princess said before turning to Pop. "What you think?"

"I don't think it make sense, like she said. Why would they kill him at home and move the body? Why would they leave his phone? It don't sound like a robbery. Somebody trynna teach a lesson."

"Gonzo? Or somebody else?"

"I can't say for sure, but I don't think so. That shit dead long as they don't know I'm in Texas. Plus, that's between me and him."

"I got the numbers," Keysha said. "The last number that called him was Trina, his friend. We don't know the last number he called, but it got a Texas area code. I'm callin' it now."

Princess and Pop watched expectantly while she called the number. The automated voice answered, saying the phone was no longer in service.

"I wonder if it's a way to find out whose number that was?" Keysha asked.

"I don't know, but I'ma look into it," Princess said. "When is Uncle Larry's funeral?"

"He ain't havin' no funeral. Since he was in the water so long, his body got fucked up and Momma had him cremated. We havin' a service at church this weekend, and then a get-together in the park later on."

"Alright. I got a coupla things to do, but I'ma be there."

"Wait. Where you goin'? You just got here."

Princess let out a long breath. "Girl, if I told you all the shit I got goin' on, yo' head would pop off. Trust me, cousin, I gotta go."

"Damn. It's that serious?"

"Yeah. It is."

Keysha wanted to know more, but she knew Princess probably wouldn't tell her. "Okay. I'll see you later. Where Queenie?"

Princess had to look away. "Honestly, I don't know. I been looking for her for a while. But if you hear from her, give her my number."

Keysha couldn't believe what she was hearing. Princess and Queenie had been inseparable their whole lives. Now one twin was missing. "Princess, what is going on? Tell me."

Princess gave her cousin an even stare. "Trust me, cousin. I'm good. For real. And don't tell nobody I'm here. Only Queenie, if you talk to her."

Keysha gave Princess a long look. "Okay. I will."

Pop Somethin' thought about Princess' uncle as he cruised the rented F-150 through traffic. The murder didn't make sense. It had to be a retaliation for something. But what?

Ten minutes later he parked the truck in front of Aunty Ruby's house. "I hope she ain't still mad at me for throwin' Drama out the window."

"Damn. I forgot about that," Princess smiled. "How much money you got on you? You know dead presidents make all wounds heal faster."

"I'ma tip her nice. She been knowin' me since I was a li'l nigga. Hopefully she ain't too mad."

After climbing from the truck, the goon and goonette walked up on the porch and rang the doorbell. A few moments later, Aunty Ruby's face appeared in the door's small window. When she seen Pop, something flashed in her eyes, but the big man wasn't sure what it was until the door opened. When he looked at her, he immediately noticed a deep sadness in her eyes.

"You okay, Aunty Ruby?"

"Hey, Paul. I guess you haven't heard."

He looked confused. "Heard what?"

"Y'all come in. We need to talk."

Doom and gloom overcame Pop as he walked into the house. "What's goin' on, Aunty?"

After closing the door, she spun to face him, the sadness in her eyes deepening. "Desmond is gone."

Pop flinched like someone had punched him. "What?"

"Yeah, nephew. He gone. Funeral in a couple days."

Pop searched the living room for something to focus on, unable to take the pain in her eyes or the sorrow filling his heart.

"What happened? How he die?" Princess asked, her eyes brimming with tears.

"He got shot. It happened in Dallas. They said he was trynna rob somebody. A couple people dead."

"You got La'Qua number?" Pop asked.

"I got it in my phone. They don't live in Houston no more. They in Dallas now."

Pop didn't waste time calling after he got the number. La'Qua picked up on the second ring. "Hello?"

"La'Qua, this Pop. I heard about Deso. Where you live? We need to holla."

"Pop, we been trynna find you for so long, nigga. We live in Dallas. I'ma text you the address. Where you at?"

"I'm at Aunty Ruby house. I got Princess wit' me. We finna hit the highway right now."

"Okay. But I gotta tell you one more thing."

"Yeah. What up?"

"Queenie here."

Pop's eyes grew several inches wider. "What you just say?"

Queenie here. Her and Shanice."

Pop's eyes grew even wider as he looked at Princess.

"What happened?" Princess asked.

"Queenie alive. She wit' La'Qua. Shanice there, too."

Princess' heart skipped a beat, her eyes growing wide as Pop's as she snatched the phone. "Hello? Queenie?"

"Nah, this La'Qua. Queenie in the back. Hold on."

Princess' body began to shake as the tears ran down her face and relief flooded her body.

"Hello? Princess?"

Princess dropped to her knees at the sound of her sister's voice. "Queenie! Oh, shit! We thought you was dead."

"Watch that language in my house, young lady," Aunty Ruby scolded.

"I'm sorry, Ms. Ruby," she apologized.

"Where you at?" Queenie asked. "Is Pop wit' you?"

"He right here. We in Houston, at Deso aunty house. We finna come to y'all. What happened? How you get out the hospital? We thought somebody kidnapped you."

"They did. Kinda. I don't wanna talk about it on the phone. But I'm okay. I been lookin' for y'all. Where y'all end up at?"

"We landed in Jacksonville, Florida. Doin' it just like old times. I'ma fill you in on everything."

***

As soon as Queenie hung up the phone, Shanice was in her face.

"So, that's it? Now that you got back in contact wit' yo' sister and Pop, that's it?"

Queenie sat up in bed to face her woman. "It's over for the plans I had wit' Pop Squad, baby girl. We already talked about this. I told you I had to get back with them. That's my family."

Shanice's face was a mask of pain. "But what about me? We not family? I love you."

"And I love you, too. You know I do. This not easy for me. If I could take you with us, I would. But I can't. I gotta go. I'm sorry."

Shanice grabbed Queenie and the women began wrestling. Queenie eventually over powered her and climbed on top, pinning her arms down.

"No, Shanice! We not about to do this. Stop! I don't wanna fight you."

Tears rolled down the sides of Shanice's face as she poured out her heart. "Please, don't leave me, Queenie. I love you. Don't go wit' him. He took everything from me already. He took my man and my baby. Don't let him take you from me, too. I can't handle losing you."

Queenie didn't want to cry, but seeing the love and pain in Shanice's eyes got to her. "C'mon, baby girl. You makin' this hard for me. You know how I feel about Pop. That's my nigga."

"But he left you to die. He just using you. He don't love you like I do. Stay with me. Please," Shanice begged.

"I can't, baby girl. I gotta go."

The women remained in the same position, crying together. It was finally over.

"Let me up. I wanna leave before he get here."

Queenie hesitated to let her go.

"I don't wanna fight no more. I know where yo' heart is. I wanna leave."

As soon as Queenie let her go, Shanice got up and began getting dressed. "Can you at least grab me a bag so I can put my clothes in?"

When Queenie left the room, Shanice found her phone and took it. When Queenie came back with garbage bags, Shanice filled them without a word. When she got everything she needed, she turned to Queenie.

"I loved you, for real. And I'ma always love you. Tell my cousin I said fuck him, and one day he gon' get what he deserves."

When Shanice left, Queenie fell backward onto the bed, breathing a sigh of relief. It was finally over.

"Why Shanice leaving?" La'Qua asked, walking in the room.

"She hate Pop Somethin'."

La'Qua frowned. "Why she hate her cousin?"

"It's a long story. Pop and Princess on the way. I leavin'."

La'Qua lay on the bed next to Queenie and wrapped her in a hug. "I know. You told us already. I don't know what I'ma do without you."

"I'm not gon' forget about you. Once I put all this other bullshit behind me, I'm comin' back to get you. You gotta get away from Drama and Snot. They ain't shit without Deso. If you keep fuckin' wit' these niggas, they gon' get you killed. Just fall back 'til I get everything situated. I'ma find you."

La'Qua let out a long sigh, tears filling her eyes. "I don't know what to do without Deso either. I miss him so much."

Queenie reached over and held her friend.

"What up wit' Shanice?" Drama asked, the gash on the side of his head shining from ointment as he walked in the room.

"She leavin'," Queenie answered. "So am I. Pop and Princess on the way."

Mistrust and anger flashed in his eyes. "So, that's it huh?"

"Why Shanice leave?" Snot asked, showing up in the doorway.

"They broke up. Pop Somethin' and Princess on the way to get Queenie," Drama explained.

Snot shot the bald woman a mean mug. "Just like that, huh? Deso and Skittlez get knocked off and you vamp, huh?"

"C'mon, man. Y'all know it ain't like that. I was all the way in with y'all. I tried to put us on top, but they got killed and we got hot."

"Y'all niggas ain't gotta do this er'time somethin' happen y'all don't like," La'Qua defended Queenie. "She did what she could. She got us up out that raggedy-ass house and put some money in our bag. What more do you niggas want? If she wanna leave, let her go. Shit, now that Deso gone, y'all need to figure out what y'all gon' do. I'm goin' back to Houston and try to get my daughter back."

Drama and Snot glared at the women angrily. All of their futures were up in the air. The young gunners had their futures attached to Deso. Now that he was gone, they weren't sure what their next move would be.

Drama was out of words, so he left the room. Snot, on the other hand, had one last warning. "That nigga ain't comin' to this house. If he do, I'm offin' his ass."

"Damn, them niggas be gettin' on my nerves!" Queenie breathed.

"They just mad and lost," La'Qua said, feeling sorry for them. "They don't know what to do without Deso. Damn, I'ma miss my nigga."

"Me, too. Deso was my nigga," Queenie said, searching for her phone. She wanted to send Pop a warning text about Drama and Snot. After looking around the room, she asked La'Qua, "You seen my phone?"

"Nah, but you need to find it so you can send that text. I don't wanna go to no more funerals."

Queenie came to the only solution. "Shanice took it. Lemme see yo' phone!"

Shanice answered on the third ring.

"Where my phone?"

"I got it," Shanice said arrogantly. "If you want it, you know how to find me."

"You betta bring back my phone. I ain't playin'."

"I'm not playin', either. I'm keepin it. And I'm goin' to my momma house. If you want it, come get it."

Queenie got pissed. "You know what, bitch? Fuck you and that phone!"

Click.

Chapter 18

Princess watched the front door without blinking, barely able to contain herself. The thought of seeing her sister after so long was unbearable. She felt like she owed somebody a 'thank you' for keeping Queenie alive. God. The universe. Good fortune. Somebody.

When the door finally opened, Queenie stepped into the Texas sun, bald head shining like she had just shaved it. Princess couldn't hold back. She let out a cry as she leapt from the passenger seat of the truck and ran to her sister. They crashed into one another and spun around in a circle, crying.

"Damn, bitch! You really cut yo' hair!" Princess cried, rubbing Queenie's bald head.

Queenie ran her fingers through Princess' dreads. "You went blue."

Pop stood near the truck, watching the sisters embrace. He was happy to see Queenie. Without hair, his bitch was still bad. He wanted to be in the middle of the display of affection, but the warning text about Drama and Snot and the shadows in the window kept him on point. So, while the sisters hugged, he stood near the driver's door, the Desert Eagle in his fist.

When the front door opened, he lifted the gun, ready to blaze.

"Chill, nigga! It's me!" La'Qua called.

"Tell them niggas to get out the window," Pop called.

"They not gon' do nothin' wit' us out here. Plus, it's broad daylight. Calm down, nigga."

After more hugs and tears, the women moved toward the truck. Queenie smiled wide as she walked toward Pop.

"My king!"

"My queen!" Pop cheesed, opening his arms.

The kiss they shared could've won an award. It was wild, passionate, and aggressive. Princess watched for a moment, a tinge of jealousy entering her heart and making her look away.

"Y'all get a muthafuckin' room!" La'Qua laughed.

"I missed you so much, baby," Queenie sang. "And I ain't had no good dick in a long time. You betta fuck me good, nigga."

"I'ma make you wet the bed," Pop grinned before giving her another peck on the lips. Then he turned to La'Qua. "I heard about Deso. That shit fucked up. You know I got you if you need anything."

La'Qua looked to the sky as tears filled her eyes, taking a few moments to blink away the pain. "Thank you, Pop."

"What happened?"

"I was in the car. Queenie know better than me."

When Pop turned to Queenie, she was looking down at the ring on his finger. "When you start wearin' rings?"

"Princess got it for me. What happened to Deso?"

Queenie spun to her sister, eyeing the ring on her finger. "I see y'all got rings an' shit. Did I miss somethin'?"

Princess shifted uncomfortably, unknowingly twisting the engagement ring on her left finger. "We thought you was gone, Queenie. These our promise rings. Nothin' won't ever break us up."

Anger and jealously flashed in Queenie's eyes as she spun to Pop, searching his face for any emotion or sign that would make her feel better.

All she got was his poker face. "We can talk about this later," Pop said flatly. "What happened to Deso?"

It took her a moment, but Queenie eventually pushed her feelings aside. "We tried to hit this nigga, Aloe. He caught me trynna let Pop Squad in and upped on me. Deso was the first one in the door and got it. We got them niggas, but Deso didn't make it."

"Is anybody lookin' for y'all? He got a team?"

"Yeah, we got a lotta niggas lookin for us, but they not plugged thugs. I think we good."

Pop turned to La'Qua. "What you gon' do? Deso was my li'l brotha, and if you ain't got nowhere to go, I got a spot for you. We in Florida fuckin' it up."

"I don't know. I was thinkin' 'bout goin' back to Houston and trynna get my daughter back."

"We gotta get her away from Drama and Snot," Queenie spoke up. "They gon' fuck around and get her killed."

"Tell you what? You comin' to Florida. If you change yo' mind, go back home. Y'all get in so we can get the fuck outta here."

"Can I go grab a bag real quick?" La'Qua asked.

"Nah. We up. You get all new shit."

When everybody hopped in the truck, Princess turned to Queenie. "Tell me how the fuck you got out the hospital. We had Tanya try to find you."

"Who is Tanya?"

"Uncle Bruce daughter. She livin' in Jacksonville. She a bad bitch, too."

Queenie thought for a moment. "Oh, I remember her. That is so crazy. And y'all might not believe this, but D.D. got me out the hospital."

Pop looked at Queenie through the rearview mirror. "Grind Squad?"

"Yeah. He kidnapped me and we made a deal. For me to live, I had to tell him where you and Princess was. But just in case I tried to play him, I had to tell him where some of the family lived. He killed Uncle Larry because he thought I was lyin' about not bein' able to find y'all."

"Bitch-ass nigga," Pop cursed.

Princess eyed Queenie like she was stupid. "Why would you tell him where our family lived?"

Queenie's anger flared. "Because I wanted to live! I didn't have a choice. I was trynna buy time to get back to y'all so we could figure it out. I wasn't layin' up, makin' promises, trynna get married an' shit. I was out here trynna survive, making power moves. I lost a lot. I took bullets for y'all, so don't make it seem like I just did some punk-ass shit. I didn't know he was gon' kill Uncle Larry. If y'all wouldn't have left me, we wouldn't be in none of this."

Princess was surprised Queenie had talked to her with so much hostility. The accusation that she left her sister to die cut deep, opening a wound that bled guilt. And as she stared into her sister's eyes, she could see a change. She couldn't put her finger on it, but something was different about Queenie. "I didn't leave you,"

Princess cried. "I tried to get to you, but Pop wouldn't let me."

"I knew we couldn't move you," Pop spoke up. "I knew the only way to save you was to let the ambulance come get you. We couldn't risk movin' you or trynna get you to the hospital. We couldn't risk gettin' locked up."

Queenie turned her anger on Pop. "So, just let me die? Sacrifice me to save y'all asses?"

"You muthafuckin' right!" Pop exploded. "That's what loyalty is. That's what love is. You been to church. You know what the preachers say about Jesus dyin' to save the whole world outta love. I tried to get you back. I killed the nigga that shot you. But I'm not goin' back to jail for nobody. And you betta get that shit outta yo' head, 'cause you ain't goin' to jail for nobody, either. You think they gon' play witchu if them white folks catch you for all the bodies you dropped? They gon' bury yo' ass, Queenie. Have you wishin' you was dead. Fuck that. I made a call, and that's what it is. If you gon' be mad at somebody, be mad at me. And then get over it. Death before dishonor, baby. Loyalty over everything."

Silence filled the cab of the truck as everyone digested the words spoken by Pop Somethin'.

From Pop Squad's hideout, Pop drove downtown to rent a hotel. The plan was to lay low until Larry's funeral, and then get back to Florida. When the foursome walked into the room, Pop went to the bathroom while the women settled around the room.

La'Qua noticed the tension between the sisters, so she busied herself with her phone. Princess sat in a chair near the window while Queenie plopped down on the bed. The twins stared at each other silently, waiting for the other to talk.

"So, y'all in love now?" Queenie asked.

"C'mon, Queenie. It ain't like that. We ain't' gettin' married or nothin'."

"But ch'all gettin' rings an' shit. You knew I loved him. I tried everything to get him to love me. You said fuck love. Now all of a sudden y'all wearin' rings. What I'm s'posed to think?"

"Pop is our nigga. I been fuckin' him just as long as you."

"You still ain't answer my question. Y'all in love?"

Princess looked away, taking a few moments to think of an answer. When she looked back at Queenie, earnest expectation was in her eyes. "Yeah. We in love. For the first time in my life, I'm in love."

Queenie cringed, the words feeling like a blow to the chest. Princess noticed the effect of her words and tried to explain. "You was gone, sis. I needed him to fill the hole you left in my soul. We thought you was dead. He was the closest thing I had to feel connected to you. I'm sorry. I didn't mean for this to happen, but this where we at."

The tears rolled silently down Queenie's face, a fire burning within her chest. "You know how I felt. I hear what you sayin', but it still hurt. I wanted him to be in love wit' me. I wanted kids wit' him. I wanted to marry him. But now he in love wit' you. And it hurt."

La'Qua watched the sisters intently, wanting to intervene, but knowing to stay quiet.

When the door opened, all eyes flocked to Pop Somethin'. He emerged butt-naked, eyes locked on Queenie. "C'mere."

She got up and walked over to stand before him.

The big man towered over her, peering down at the bald woman like he was her god. He brought the pinky ring to her face, giving her a good look at it. "You see this? I got it from Princess. This a symbol of her dedication to me. And the ring she got is a symbol of my dedication to her. We past bein' niggas and bitches. She part of me, and I'm part of her. We are one. I love her and she love me. I would sacrifice myself for her, and vice versa. You got a problem wit' that, say what you need to say."

Queenie didn't hesitate. "I love you, Pop. You knew that. And I tried everything to get you to love me. But you wouldn't. And now I get back and find out you love my sister. That shit hurt, and I'm mad about it. I was down witchu from the minute we first met. If you should be lovin' anybody, it should be me."

Pop nodded in agreement. "You right, and I respect how you feel. And I want you to know I love you, too. When we thought you died, you took a part of us. We bonded over that, and it brought us closer. And now that you back, that bond is shared by all of us. Queenie, we love you. We are one, like a three-stranded rope. This ring don't matter to me. What matter is those bullets you took for me. You sacrificed yo'self for me. That's love. C'mere, Princess. Gimme that ring."

When Princess handed Pop the ring, he went in the bathroom and flushed it down the toilet. "We don't need jewelry to show what we already know. Instead, we gon' do it how they did it back in the day. We gon' get branded. I'ma go first. I know one of y'all got tweezers in them purses."

After getting the tweezers from Princess, Pop took off his ring and used the tweezers to hold it over the fire from a lighter. When it was blazing, he touched it to the left side of his chest, above his heart. He repeated the process three times, branding interconnected rings like an Olympic sign. Then he did the same thing to Princess and Queenie.

La'Qua sat at the table watching everything, unsure what she should do. "So, if I stay, do I gotta get that, too? Shit look like it hurt."

"Nah. To be all the way down, you gotta have a trial by fire. This another level of loyalty. This ain't for you. Yet," Pop said before turning to his women. "Now it's official. I love both of y'all equally. We all pieces of each other. We ain't fightin' over who loves who. We are one. Y'all good?"

Princess nodded before turning to Queenie. "You good?"

Queenie smiled, satisfied by the display of love and devotion. "I'm good. And I'm sorry for gettin' all emotional. I love y'all, and those rings had me feelin' left out. But I'm good now. We are one."

Pop smiled. "Now let's kiss and make up. Princess, let me and Queenie get this first round so I can show her what she been missin'."

"Get her, baby!" Princess smiled.

Pop shoved Queenie onto the bed roughly before climbing on top. After a wild tongue kiss, he nibbled his way down her neck to her breasts. Queenie's nipples were black as night, poking out like hard, black diamonds. He took the left one in his mouth, sucking and flicking his tongue across the top. Queenie moaned her approval. After a few moments, he went to the right one and gave it the same attention before licking his way down to her waist. Instead of attacking her pussy, Pop focused on her inner thighs, kissing, licking, and sucking the erogenous zone.

"Oh yeah, baby!" Queenie moaned, grabbing a fistful of his dreads. "That feels so good!"

After a few more minutes of foreplay, Pop finally moved to her pussy. It was clean shaven, her lips plump and engorged with blood. He licked the labia from top to bottom a few times, Queenie sucking in deep breaths of air, loving the attention Pop was paying her body.

After tasting her juices, he used his thumbs to spread the lips apart, exposing her clitoris. His tongue became a blur as it flicked across her pearl.

"Oh shit, Pop! Oh shit!"

He switched back and forth from sucking and licking her clit, then stuffed two fingers in her pussy and one in her ass. When Queenie came, the orgasm blew through her body like a typhoon, taking her breath away. Pop didn't even let her catch her breath before jumping on top and shoving his meat into her still-spasming pussy. He threw her legs on his shoulders, beginning with short, slow strokes, allowing her to adjust to him being in her walls again.

"Oh, muthafucka! Shit!" Queenie moaned, digging her nails into his shoulders.

"You want some more?" he asked. "Tell me how bad you want my dick."

A mix of pleasure and pain shown on Queenie's face and in her eyes. "Quit playin' wit' me, nigga. I want all that dick. Fuck me hard."

A grin as wide as the Joker's spread across Pop's face as he deepened his strokes and sped up his pace. His pelvis slammed against hers every time he pushed forward, making a slapping noise. He beat up the pussy, showing no mercy.

Queenie screamed in ecstasy, loving the drilling by her man.

When he was about to nut, he pulled out of her and aggressively rolled her onto her stomach. He grabbed a pillow and slid it under her pelvis, lifting her ass in the air a little. Then he was back at it, long-stroking his woman into sexual bliss. Her ass bounced and jiggled violently as he pounded her pussy from behind.

Queenie came in a rush, her vaginal walls squeezing his dick, making his nut come faster than he wanted.

"Aw, shit!" he grunted as he snatched out and busted on her ass and lower back.

"Damn!" La'Qua moaned. "Y'all muthafuckas got me horny as fuck!"

"I wanna get fucked like that!" Princess added.

Pop looked over his shoulder at the horny women. "Quit standin on the sideline and get in the game. It's enough of me to go around."

Chapter 19

Drama sat on the couch playing with the .40 caliber Smith and Wesson, clicking the safety on and off. He had been sitting in the same spot for twenty minutes, the same thoughts passing through his mind. "We shoulda blazed his ho-ass when he was standin' in front of the house."

Snot sat across from his war brother puffing a blunt of loud, the words echoing through his head like he spoke them. "All them muthafuckas gon' be pushin' flowers, brah. La'Qua bitch-ass, too. I can't believe she hit it wit' that nigga. That shit was disloyal, fam."

"On what Breezy wasn't spittin' the truth when he said these hos ain't loyal?" Drama agreed. "We should go to that funeral and get they ho-asses."

Snot looked up at his boy like he had just solved a Rubik's Cube. "Won't nobody expect that, brah. We can lick all they asses at the same time."

Drama dialed back his enthusiasm about shooting up the funeral when he seen how serious Snot was. "I was just sayin' that shit, mane. You know how many people gon' be at that funeral? You know a muthafucka prolly gon' be recordin' that shit. I want all they bitch-asses dead, but a funeral, mane? I don't think we should make that move."

Snot sat up straight, eyeing Drama intently. "Brah, that's the perfect time! We can wear disguises and blend in. Get some of La'Qua wigs and some big-ass glasses. We can do it, my nigga."

Drama didn't look convinced. "I don't know, mane. That shit hot as fuck."

"We always been hot, nigga. We been takin' these penitentiary chances since we started fuckin' niggas over. We bring heat to niggas no matter where they at, mornin', noon, or night. If Deso was here and these wasn't muthafuckas he fucked wit', you know he'da be ready to make this move. This our shot, brah. They won't see us comin'."

Drama seen the eagerness to spill blood in his brother's eyes. It was true they had gotten down on niggas at all times of the day, and now they had an opportunity to silence four enemies in one shot. The opportunity to get Pop Somethin' might not even fall into their laps again. "Fuck it. This might be our only chance to get this nigga. How we gon' find out where the funeral at?"

Snot smiled. "I got it. I'ma call La'Qua all sad an' shit. She gon' let that shit slip. Watch. All they bitch-asses gettin' mopped up, brah. We gon' turn that funeral into a massacre!"

***

Shanice lay in bed with her daughter watching cartoons. The bouncing toddler was snuggled up next to her mother, loving the attention she got from the most important person in her small world.

"Momma, do you think you can see love?"

Shanice looked down at the spitting image of herself, surprised by the question. "Why you ask me that?"

"Because everybody always say 'I love you,' but how do you know it's real if you can't see it?"

Shanice laughed aloud, amused by the child's question. "How long you been thinking about this?"

"Ever since you came back home. You said you loved me, but you left me for a long time. I was mad at you. Do you really love me?"

"Yes, I really love you, Shawntale. And you know this because I make sacrifices for you. I take care of you. I provide for you. I feed you and clean up after you. And when you was a baby, I had to wipe all your no-no spots because you couldn't do it yourself. Love is an action word. You can't see love, but you can see if people love you by what they do for you."

"What about Daddy? He gone to Heaven. If he really loved me, why he leave?"

"Daddy didn't have a choice, baby. God took him to Heaven. God can take whoever he wants, whenever he wants. And it ain't nothing nobody can do about it. But just because he left don't mean Daddy didn't love you. He loved you as much as I do."

"What about Queenie? She said she loved me and you, but she gone now. Did she really love us? And why do everybody that love us keep leaving?"

Shanice was momentarily thrown by the question. It opened a wound that was still healing, and the way Shawntale stared up at her told she was awaiting an answer. "Queenie loves us, too, but she had some really important things to take care of."

"When is she coming back? Can I call her?"

"I don't know when she's coming back. She might not ever."

"So, can we call her. I miss her, Mommy."

Shanice looked toward the phone that lay on the dresser. It was Queenie's. "No. We can't call her. I don't have her number. But when she calls, I'ma make sure to let her know you want to talk to her."

"Okay, Mommy. You know I love you, right?"

Shanice smiled at her daughter, planting a kiss on her forehead. "And I love you, too, baby."

When Shawntale turned back to the TV, Shanice's mind stayed on Queenie. She missed the bald-headed woman. Her body burned to be touched by her dark skin. She had never loved anyone as much as she loved Queenie. She would do anything for that woman. Sacrifice anything. Everything. But she was still in love with Pop Somethin'. The man Shanice hated. The man who single-handedly destroyed her last two attempts at happiness. He killed her C-Note and her baby, and almost got Queenie killed. But nothing bad ever happened to him. All he did was bring pain. The world would be a better place without him in it. If only there was a way to get rid of him. Then she could get Queenie back. But how? He had enemies everywhere but no one could touch him. She wished Queenie had told D.D. where he was. Then she wouldn't be lying in bed lovesick. She would have her woman in her arms and they would be planning their future. But Pop had ruined that. And he needed to pay.

That's when she remembered Queenie's phone. She jumped out of the bed so fast she got lightheaded.

"You okay, Mommy?" Shawntale asked.

"Yeah. I'm fine. I just need to make a call," she said, powering on the phone and scrolling the call logs. When she found the name she was looking for, her heart rate increased and palms began to sweat. The problem-solver was literally at her fingertips. But could she handle the blood being on her hands?

Then she thought of everything Pop had taken from her and pressed call.

He answered on the fourth ring. "You betta have that location for me, Queenie. Next time I hit, I'm takin' more than one."

"Um. This not Queenie," Shanice stuttered. "Is this D.D.?"

"What the fuck is this? Don't be playin' on my phone!"

"Um. I can't tell you my name, but I know where Pop Somethin' is."

There was a slight pause before D.D. spoke again. "Who is this? How you know I'm lookin' for Pop Somethin'?"

"I can't tell you who I am, but I'm a friend of Queenie's. She with Pop Somethin' right now."

"Okay. Where they at?"

"Wait. Before I tell you this, you need to promise me one thing. The only way I'ma tell you where they at is if you promise not to touch Queenie. I need her to live."

D.D. laughed. "I know who you is now. You her girl she was fightin' wit' the last time I called. Okay, stranger, I'ma play yo' game. I won't touch her. On one condition. Tell me if I'm right. You her girl. You mad she wit' him?"

Shanice was surprised at how easily he figured it all out. "Yeah. She my girl. And Pop took her. I want her back."

"So we got somethin' in common, because Pop Somethin' took somethin from me, too. My brother. Okay. I won't touch Queenie. That's my word. Where he at?"

"Her uncle's funeral is tomorrow. In Houston. When I find out the location, I'ma text it to you. Please, just don't hurt my girl."

"You got my word, stranger. I'm a fair-minded businessman, and I honor my word. Send me that text."

***

Pop Somethin' hated churches. Being surrounded by sadness and fake Christians made him uneasy. He watched in amusement as the preacher gave the eulogy, the choir sang, and family members got up to the pulpit to speak on Uncle Larry's virtues. He wished he hadn't agreed to come. The only good thing was they would hop on the highway immediately after the repast.

Two hours later, family members kissed and hugged as they began filing out of the church. Pop, Queenie, Princess, and La'Qua were mixed in the crowd. As soon as Pop stepped into the Houston sun, the hair on the back of his neck stood up and goosebumps crawled all over his skin. His instincts had been honed by the streets and were akin to Spiderman's Spidey Senses. Something was wrong. Danger was near. He could feel it.

His trigger finger twitched as the .50-caliber burned on his hip like it had a mind of its own, desiring to be pulled out and popped.

"Somethin' ain't right. Be on the lookout," he told the women as his eyes darted back and forth over the family members, parked cars, and nearby buildings, searching for the cause of his discomfort.

"What you talkin' 'bout?" Queenie asked, picking up on his mood and keeping her eyes peeled.

"I don't know. I got a feelin'. I told you not to leave yo' shit in the truck. Hurry up and get to the rental."

The F-150 was parked halfway down the block. Before they could get to it, Pop spotted the danger. Two tall, skinny, dark-skinned niggas wore wigs and sunglasses, trying to look like women. He knew it was Drama and Snot. They were a few hundred feet away, moving toward them, reaching under their shirts.

"There they go! Look out!" Pop called, pointing them out as he reached for the .50.

Tat-tat-tat-tat-tat-tat-tat-tat-tat-tat-tat-tat-tat-tat-tat!

Fully automatic gunfire rang out, exploding the windows of the car Pop and his girls were walking by.

As he ducked for cover, out the corner of his eye Pop could see someone dressed in black stepping out of a black Caravan parked in the middle of the street, firing a chopper. Another figure was getting out behind him, also carrying a chopper. In the driver's seat was a masked man firing a Mac 12.

In front of him, Drama and Snot had pulled pistols, but the gunfire across the street made them pause. And that was their mistake. The Desert Eagle roared like a lion, sending hot shit faster than the speed of sound at the Pop Squad members. Snot's thin frame was lifted off the ground when two pieces of lead slammed into his chest.

Drama ducked behind a nearby truck. Pop assessed the situation quickly, not missing a beat. He needed another gun, so he turned and threw Princess the Desert Eagle. "Knock 'em down, baby! Get 'em off my ass!"

Princess didn't hesitate. She came up from behind the car, letting the .50 caliber ride. The hand cannon exploded high-powered rounds toward the shooters near the van. The lead man caught bullets in the leg, stomach, and chest before falling to the ground.

As soon as Princess began letting loose, Pop sprinted toward Snot's fallen body, eyeing the pistol at his side.

He was a few feet away when Drama jumped out from behind the truck, his pistol high. When he seen Pop racing toward him and realized the big man would be upon him before he could aim at him, he flinched and squeezed the trigger. The bullet whistled by Pop Somethin' and hit Princess in the neck as she was ducking for cover.

Reacting on pure instinct, Pop lowered his shoulder and crashed into the smaller man like he was making a football play. Drama was lifted in the air and thrown a few feet before crashing to the ground.

Right after making the tackle, Pop did a tuck-roll, grabbing the pistol Snot dropped, cocking it, and sending a bullet flying from the chamber as he hit the safety. When he hopped back to his feet again, the pistol was erupting fire toward the shooters near the minivan.

The second man with the chopper never knew what hit him as a bullet smacked his temple, sending brains and gray matter spraying into the air.

Before he could get a bead on the driver, Pop had to duck again as Drama took aim at him. The bullets missed, slamming into the parked car. And that's when Pop seen Princess. She was lying on Queenie's lap, bleeding from the neck. Instant pain gripped his chest, feeling like he had been shot.

The sound of an engine revving and tires screeching pulled his attention away from his women as the Caravan sped away. After peeking his head from behind the car, he seen Drama was gone, too. When he looked to his girls again, Queenie was wailing at the top of her lungs while La'Qua lay on the ground, bleeding. Without even seeing her face, Pop knew Princess was gone. He felt it. The regret of coming back to Houston began to weigh on him.

He had taken two steps toward his girls when the hair on the back of his neck stood up again. The pistol was a blur as he spun around, applying pressure to the trigger. When he recognized who was standing behind him, a mix of emotions flashed through him. "What the fuck you doin' here?" he growled, lowering the gun. "I almost killed yo' ass."

Shanice stood before Pop with a determined look on her face. "I want Queenie back."

"What the fuck you talkin' 'bout? Get outta here, right now," Pop snapped before turning to walk away.

"Paul!"

Hearing his government name made him freeze. He spun around and was shocked to see Shanice pointing a gun at him. When he looked in her eyes, pain, anger, and hate blazed at him. He no longer recognized her as his favorite little cousin that he was secretly in love with. The woman before him was a stranger.

"You took everything from me. Now I'm taking everything from you."

Even though he knew he wouldn't be able to shoot her before she squeezed the trigger, Pop tried to lift the gun anyway.

Pop, pop!

One bullet pierced his chest, the other his neck as he fell backwards to the ground.

The last thing Pop Somethin' remembered was feeling the sting of bloody betrayal.

The End

Submission Guideline

Submit the first three chapters of your completed manuscript to ldpsubmissions@gmail.com, subject line: Your book's title. The manuscript must be in a .doc file and sent as an attachment. Document should be in Times New Roman, double spaced and in size 12 font. Also, provide your synopsis and full contact information. If sending multiple submissions, they must each be in a separate email.

Have a story but no way to send it electronically? You can still submit to LDP/Ca$h Presents. Send in the first three chapters, written or typed, of your completed manuscript to:

LDP: Submissions Dept
Po Box 870494
Mesquite, Tx 75187

DO NOT send original manuscript. Must be a duplicate.

Provide your synopsis and a cover letter containing your full contact information.

Thanks for considering LDP and Ca$h Presents.

J-Blunt

Coming Soon from Lock Down Publications/Ca$h Presents

BOW DOWN TO MY GANGSTA

By **Ca$h**

TORN BETWEEN TWO

By **Coffee**

BLOOD STAINS OF A SHOTTA **III**

By **Jamaica**

STEADY MOBBIN **III**

By **Marcellus Allen**

BLOOD OF A BOSS **V**

By **Askari**

LOYAL TO THE GAME **IV**

LIFE OF SIN II

By **T.J. & Jelissa**

A DOPEBOY'S PRAYER **II**

By **Eddie "Wolf" Lee**

IF LOVING YOU IS WRONG... **III**

LOVE ME EVEN WHEN IT HURTS **II**

By **Jelissa**

TRUE SAVAGE **VII**

By **Chris Green**

BLAST FOR ME **III**

A BRONX TALE III

DUFFLE BAG CARTEL II

By **Ghost**

ADDICTIED TO THE DRAMA **III**

By **Jamila Mathis**

LIPSTICK KILLAH **III**

Mimi

A Gangster's Code 3

WHAT BAD BITCHES DO **III**

A HUSTLER'S DECEIT 3

KILL ZONE **II**

By **Aryanna**

THE COST OF LOYALTY **II**

By **Kweli**

SHE FELL IN LOVE WITH A REAL ONE **II**

By **Tamara Butler**

RENEGADE BOYS **III**

By **Meesha**

CORRUPTED BY A GANGSTA **IV**

By **Destiny Skai**

A GANGSTER'S CODE **III**

By **J-Blunt**

KING OF NEW YORK IV

RISE TO POWER III

By **T.J. Edwards**

GORILLAS IN THE BAY II

De'Kari

THE STREETS ARE CALLING II

Duquie Wilson

KINGPIN KILLAZ III

Hood Rich

STEADY MOBBIN' **III**

Marcellus Allen

SINS OF A HUSTLA II

ASAD

TRIGGADALE II

Elijah R. Freeman

MARRIED TO A BOSS II

J-Blunt

By Destiny Skai & Chris Green
KINGS OF THE GAME II
Playa Ray

<u>**Available Now**</u>
<u>RESTRAINING ORDER **I & II**</u>
By **CA$H & Coffee**
<u>LOVE KNOWS NO BOUNDARIES **I II & III**</u>
By **Coffee**
<u>RAISED AS A GOON I, II, III & IV</u>
<u>BRED BY THE SLUMS I, II, III</u>
<u>BLAST FOR ME I & II</u>
<u>ROTTEN TO THE CORE I III</u>
<u>A BRONX TALE I, II</u>
By **Ghost**
<u>LAY IT DOWN **I & II**</u>
<u>LAST OF A DYING BREED</u>
<u>BLOOD STAINS OF A SHOTTA I & II</u>
By **Jamaica**
<u>LOYAL TO THE GAME</u>
<u>LOYAL TO THE GAME II</u>
<u>LOYAL TO THE GAME III</u>
<u>LIFE OF SIN</u>
By **TJ & Jelissa**
<u>BLOODY COMMAS I & II</u>
<u>SKI MASK CARTEL I II & III</u>
<u>KING OF NEW YORK I II,III</u>
<u>RISE TO POWER I II</u>
By **T.J. Edwards**

194

IF LOVING HIM IS WRONG...I & II

LOVE ME EVEN WHEN IT HURTS

By **Jelissa**

WHEN THE STREETS CLAP BACK I & II III

By **Jibril Williams**

A DISTINGUISHED THUG STOLE MY HEART I II & III

LOVE SHOULDN'T HURT I II III

RENEGADE BOYS I & II

By **Meesha**

A GANGSTER'S CODE I & II

By J-Blunt

PUSH IT TO THE LIMIT

By **Bre' Hayes**

BLOOD OF A BOSS **I, II, III & IV**

By **Askari**

THE STREETS BLEED MURDER **I, II & III**

THE HEART OF A GANGSTA I II& III

By **Jerry Jackson**

CUM FOR ME

CUM FOR ME 2

CUM FOR ME 3

CUM FOR ME 4

An **LDP Erotica Collaboration**

BRIDE OF A HUSTLA **I II & II**

THE FETTI GIRLS **I, II& III**

CORRUPTED BY A GANGSTA I, II & III

By **Destiny Skai**

WHEN A GOOD GIRL GOES BAD

By **Adrienne**

A GANGSTER'S REVENGE **I II III & IV**

THE BOSS MAN'S DAUGHTERS
THE BOSS MAN'S DAUGHTERS II
THE BOSSMAN'S DAUGHTERS III
THE BOSSMAN'S DAUGHTERS IV
THE BOSS MAN'S DAUGHTERS **V**
A SAVAGE LOVE **I & II**
BAE BELONGS TO ME
A HUSTLER'S DECEIT I, II, III
WHAT BAD BITCHES DO I, II
By **Aryanna**
A KINGPIN'S AMBITON
A KINGPIN'S AMBITION **II**
I MURDER FOR THE DOUGH
By **Ambitious**
TRUE SAVAGE
TRUE SAVAGE II
TRUE SAVAGE **III**
TRUE SAVAGE **IV**
TRUE SAVAGE **V**
TRUE SAVAGE **VI**
By **Chris Green**
A DOPEBOY'S PRAYER
By **Eddie "Wolf" Lee**
THE KING CARTEL **I, II & III**
By **Frank Gresham**
THESE NIGGAS AIN'T LOYAL **I, II & III**
By **Nikki Tee**
GANGSTA SHYT **I II &III**
By **CATO**
THE ULTIMATE BETRAYAL

A Gangster's Code 3

By **Phoenix**
BOSS'N UP **I , II & III**
By **Royal Nicole**
I LOVE YOU TO DEATH
By **Destiny J**
I RIDE FOR MY HITTA
I STILL RIDE FOR MY HITTA
By **Misty Holt**
LOVE & CHASIN' PAPER
By **Qay Crockett**
TO DIE IN VAIN
SINS OF A HUSTLA
By **ASAD**
BROOKLYN HUSTLAZ
By **Boogsy Morina**
BROOKLYN ON LOCK I & II
By **Sonovia**
GANGSTA CITY
By **Teddy Duke**
A DRUG KING AND HIS DIAMOND I & II III
A DOPEMAN'S RICHES
HER MAN, MINE'S TOO I, II
CASH MONEY HO'S
By **Nicole Goosby**
TRAPHOUSE KING **I II & III**
KINGPIN KILLAZ
By **Hood Rich**
LIPSTICK KILLAH **I, II**
CRIME OF PASSION I & II
By **Mimi**

STEADY MOBBN' **I, II**

By **Marcellus Allen**

WHO SHOT YA **I, II**

Renta

GORILLAZ IN THE BAY

DE'KARI

TRIGGADALE

Elijah R. Freeman

GOD BLESS THE TRAPPERS I, II, III

THESE SCANDALOUS STREETS I, II, III

FEAR MY GANGSTA I, II, III

THESE STREETS DON'T LOVE NOBODY I, II

BURY ME A G I, II, III, IV, V

Tranay Adams

THE STREETS ARE CALLING

Duquie Wilson

MARRIED TO A BOSS…

By **Destiny Skai & Chris Green**

KINGS OF THE GAME II

Playa Ray

BOOKS BY LDP'S CEO, CA$H

TRUST IN NO MAN

TRUST IN NO MAN 2

TRUST IN NO MAN 3

BONDED BY BLOOD

SHORTY GOT A THUG

THUGS CRY

THUGS CRY 2

THUGS CRY 3

TRUST NO BITCH

TRUST NO BITCH 2

TRUST NO BITCH 3

TIL MY CASKET DROPS

RESTRAINING ORDER

RESTRAINING ORDER 2

IN LOVE WITH A CONVICT

Coming Soon

BONDED BY BLOOD 2

BOW DOWN TO MY GANGSTA

J-Blunt